Danny Boy

Also in this series

Danny Boy

James Bradner

Longman

Longman Group Limited
Longman House,
Burnt Mill, Harlow, Essex, UK

First published 1981

ISBN 0 582 78536 7

Printed in Great Britain by
Richard Clay (The Chaucer Press) Ltd,
Bungay, Suffolk

Carry the cross patiently, and with perfect submission; and in the end it shall carry you.

Thomas à Kempis

The author wishes to acknowledge his appreciation of the editorial advice, encouragement and help given him by Charlotte Rolfe in the preparation of this manuscript.

1

Horatio, the village stray, yawned, his tongue arching and stretching, his gums tautening, then falling at the sides of his mouth in two black and red scalloped loops. Through a bloodshot eye he watched the mourners dispersing until only three men remained standing in the bleak cemetery. Near a rotting tree stump, his hooves slurping in the sap, grazed a black, sore-infested bull. His tail which was bare except for several bristles at the tip, flicked at pestering flies while he chewed the bedewed grass with lethargic efforts. Large ribs, and two church-steeple flank bones betrayed the fierceness of that battle-scarred head – the soup-bone type that abbatoirs slaughter surreptitiously. The evening was otherwise a study in still-life.

Occasionally the bull would lift its twisted horns to stare vacantly at the men. Green threads of slime dangled from its mouth. Close beside the beast stalked two cattle egrets, their buff-coloured crowns sliding backwards and forwards with each delicate step. A tiny wren hopped nervously nearby, eyeing the giant herbivorous thing with considerable suspicion.

The earth was soft from previous rainfall and scores of animal tracks were clearly visible, patterning the ground. The two men eased the cripple back into a wheelchair that could justifiably have been the graveyard's *memento mori*, for it cast an ominous shadow on the grave. *Charles Savory*, read the inscription, *born 12.1.1910, died 4.10.1957. May he rest in peace*.

This new, chalk-white tomb lay conspicuous amid a dozen mud graves; graves long since forgotten with worn, termite-eaten, tumbledown crosses scattered like scarecrows which had barely survived time's elements and were on the verge of collapse.

Gold diggers, adventurers, unknown souls were buried here and unmarked graves crowned their anonymity. Below the stout wooden staves that fenced in the small burial-ground, the earth sloped into a natural trough, and the stagnant water mirrored the leaves above. Every villager confessed that here Ben's brother would repose peacefully.

Oscar glanced at his wristwatch, then at Serwall, Mahdia's schoolteacher, and with signs of the eyes and head they agreed to leave the cemetery. The sun, slipping behind the forest trees, fired many golden beams overhead. They wasted no time, for mosquitoes had already started their chorus and soon the three were slapping madly at themselves.

Wheeling the cripple, Oscar adjusted his pace as they descended the narrow, muddy hillside. Here a few candleflies sparked over sage and bramble bush, and the shrill crescendos of cicadas murdered all other sounds. Behind them an Indian lad shrieked 'Hi-ah! hi-ah!' and his whip sounded with sharp authority as hooves pounded towards familiar pens. Light began to flicker in houses, and many treetops were already enveloped in a mist which was quickly erasing elongated shadows and colour from the village scene.

The two men chatted animatedly, in the hope of cheering up the cripple but evidently Ben hadn't the heart to appreciate such goodwill. Finally, they arrived at Ben's bungalow. Puffing and panting, they lifted man and wheelchair on to the verandah, and waited until he had wheeled himself in.

Oscar shook his head ruefully and muttered, 'A bubble, vapour, shadow, fleeting dream.'

'What?'

'Oh, just something someone wrote about life. I simply can't believe Charles is dead.'

'I know what you mean,' said Serwall, 'only too well.'

They proceeded briskly up the road, the gravel crunching under their shoes. As they neared a corner, the sound of running feet was heard approaching and, on the turn, a form came flying out of the night only to collide with Oscar who cried, 'Hey, watch it!'

' 'Night, dad, 'night, Mr Serwall,' panted the intruder, hugging Oscar and swinging on and about his hips playfully. They had to laugh.

'Danny seems to like these bloodsuckers,' Serwall said, catching a mosquito with a blind sweep of the hand.

Oscar squeezed the boy's shoulder gently, 'Mr Serwall's right, son, we should be indoors.'

'See you in the morning,' said Serwall, and disappeared into the dark. Several fires, composed of dry grass, coconut husks, twigs, rubbish, and green leaves for thick smoke – to discourage mosquitoes and sandflies – blazed in the open, and the flames played with the night; now bending low; now leaping to illuminate overhead ivies; now snapping, hissing and popping musically. The smoke conspired with the night to anaesthetise the trees, for all around, like drunkards, they leaned heavily on one another. Soon the darkness was alive with bats, moths, salamanders and a host of other nocturnal creatures; marauding, hunting, mating, or wildly traversing the sky. Sometimes a pair of wings would flutter by, brushing your face, as if in memory of the macabre. Only the witches were absent from this Walpurgis Night setting.

Oversized toads flopped clumsily everywhere, and from hidden waterholes bulbous-eyed frogs roll-called sonorously, as if the very night depended on their incantations. Over in the south the heavens rumbled, and black satin drapes billowed and coiled before dim, trembling stars.

Through their white wicket-gate and up the gravelled walk trotted Oscar and his coloured foster son. Once inside the cottage they made to pull ludicrous faces at the riotous mosquitoes fighting against the panes, when the odour of cake arrested their attention.

Danny rushed into the kitchen and discovered the pan in the sink, its contents charred, but Oscar – suspecting the cause of the mishap – found Rosita in the bedroom with a thwarted expression on her face. He sat down beside her.

'Don't tell me you're cracking up because of one stupid cake!'

'I – I don't know what happened. One minute it looked perfect, and the next – oh, Oscar, what am I going to do?'

For weeks Danny had been soliloquising about the size and description of the cake he wanted, with icing an inch thick... .

'Well, it's only the fourth you've ruined.'

'You're making fun of me!'

'No, but into everyone's life some rain must fall.'

'Be serious! What are we going to give Danny?'

'Sugar and spice, ...' He ducked to avoid a pillow, but she caught his wrist and pulled him back on to the bed, determinedly revengeful.

'Take this!' she stormed, rising on her knees and tickling him until he lay helpless with laughter.

The noise issuing from their bedroom amused Danny; he sank to the floor with a book to wonder why some insects were so fascinated by a man-made light when they had all day to drool over the sun.

Oscar and Rosita lay holding hands; he looking up at the ceiling, she guessing at his thoughts.

'Oscar.'

'Huh?'

'Thinking about Danny's gift?'

'No. I'm worried about Ben.'

'Ben?'

'Uh-huh.'

'Well,' she drew nearer, 'God knows best.'

'Oh, sure.'

'Do you think we'll always be like this?'

He glanced at her. 'How?'

'Happy, I mean.'

' 'Course. Why not?'

She pressed her cheek against his arm, slipped two fingers through his shirt, and clipped affectionately at the black hairs on his chest. 'Even though I can't bear a child?'

'Nonsense! Of course we'll be happy. That doesn't bother me in the least.' He turned, cupped her small face in his hands and kissed her. Tears welled up in her eyes.

'I – I'm sorry I'm such a fool,' she muttered.

A sudden shower of rain succeeded the second rumble. Danny dropped the book, rushed into his room, slid for the hundredth time on the oval rug, caught himself on the iron bed rail, then proceeded with an exaggerated limp to shut the window. All in vain, for the downpour ended abruptly. He wanted to swear, but noticed the statue of Our Lady, sealed his lips, and contented himself by looking up at the heavens furiously. Then, through the rain-washed pane, he caught sight of her. She stood on the threshold of a cottage only a stone's throw from his window. His heart started to thump. It was she … Lily!

He tore off his shirt, changed his pants, and tripped as he tried to pull one trouser leg up both feet. After some confusion he managed to extract a leg and completed the operation, only to discover that the fly zip was at the back! Fuming, he peeled off the denims, and this time made certain he got it right. Then he pulled on his soft shoes, and hurried out.

Rosita and Oscar were conversing in the hall when he headed for the back door. They looked up in surprise. Danny not moping over his cake? Oscar sniggered.

'Who can follow the mind of a boy.'

'I thought he'd be upset.'

'Not to worry. I may have a solution.'

Rosita's eyes dilated. 'Oho, no wonder. All that secrecy with Peter yesterday. You were asking him to get something from Bartica, weren't you?'

He looked away, at the curtains, the bookshelves, the table.

'Come on, out with it!'

Still he sat obstinate.

'All right,' she smiled mischievously, 'I'll give you something really nice for your secret.' And she unzipped her dress right there in the hall.

'Rosita! Are you mad?'

'Well, tell me, otherwise …' And she threatened to slip the dress off her shoulders.

'Rosita! Danny may rush in here any minute!'

'Well, tell me.'

'No!' He opened his eyes on her. Rosita thought it prudent to quit her act.

'P-l-e-a-s-e,' she tried.

'No.'

'Oh, all right. Still, you're the sweetest man I know. However would I have faced Danny otherwise?'

He looked into her hazel eyes, at her thick eyelashes, and kissed her softly.

'Oh ye of little faith.'

'Yes, darling.'

After the funeral, Morna Welsh cleaned her shoes, showered, and went to purchase teabags. Morris had been away prospecting for months, and she eagerly awaited his return. Their house was situated beneath Pepper Hill, concealed from view by two gigantic mora. She was about to open the door when a figure issued from the shadows.

'Oh, you startled me!'

'I'm sorry, ma'am, but I – I must talk to you.'

'Look, I've told you before. I'm married, and my husband is a very jealous man!'

'I – I only wanted to give you this. I've been saving to buy it for a long time. Please ... open it.' The parcel boasted a colourful bow.

'You're crazy,' she cried, unwrapping the gift. 'This is expensive perfume!'

'What's money to one staggering in a desert of loneliness?' Two tears glistened in the night, and the noble countenance of Rudolph humbled itself before Morna's alluring beauty. She stood looking down at him, perplexed, the woman all Mahdia agreed was Marilyn Monroe recreated in bronze. Even Oscar, who was never known to be 'interested' in women, conceded that Rosita had looked like that 'a couple of years ago.'

'I can't accept this,' Morna stammered, adding, 'Look, I – I know how you feel, but I – I couldn't dream of cheating on Morris – ever! I honour my marriage.'

Rudolph could have been a puppy begging for an owner, the way he reclined at the foot of the stairs. Weakly he began to profess his love: how she was slowly tearing him to pieces with her cruel neglect; how he dreamed only of gazing into her bewitching eyes.

'Look, I'll pay you for the perfume, that's the only way.'

'Then I'll destroy myself!'

'Oh, Rudolph, you're making it hard for me. Besides, you – you're ... well, I could almost be your mother.'

His tears fell at her feet as he implored her not to abandon him, and his plaintive entreaties bore down upon her like a great, guilty conscience. He stood as if expecting the death sentence, and his hopelessness moved her deeply. He swore that her friendship was all he craved.

Gradually, she descended the stairs, until their heads were on a level, her maternal heart yielding at his apparent agony. For breathless seconds neither spoke, but remorse continued to hack away at her defences and, trembling, she lifted his chin till she could feel the warmth of his breath.

'Please understand,' she pleaded, 'I'm not that kind of woman.'

Despite her better judgement, she closed her eyes and offered her lips which he accepted gratefully. It started to rain. She pulled away.

'You'd better go.'

'No.'

'You'll get soaked.'

'An empty heart feels nothing.'

'Oh, please go.'

'No. You go, I'll leave after you shut the door.'

The rain came harder now. She faltered:

'Would you like some tea?'

Meekly, he accepted, the fabled wolf, and the impetus deceit swept Morna Welsh into a world of commiseration. Nor did the fleece wear thin till he had destroyed her every defence, and left her ashamed of her vulnerability. After he left, she kept remembering his triumphant sneer, and felt nothing for herself but total abhorrence.

After Fieldor returned from Georgetown he drove directly to his shop and opened it to replace his stock. No sooner had he done so, he got the shock of his life. Charles dead? And buried?

Fieldor was considered a man of business who never pried into the affairs of even those who were considerably indebted to him – a man not easily ruffled. But he had only been absent four days, and this!

'How did it happen?'

Explanations were proffered until Fieldor decided he had better see Ben. He looked at the men, glanced at his shelves and said, 'Keep and eye on the shop, I'll only be a minute.'

He picked up his felt hat. The pork-knockers moved to the entrance to watch as he lengthened his strides towards the bungalow, his head bent, one hand holding his hat to prevent it blowing off.

'Ah tell you-all he ain' gon believe we,' said one.

'Well,' put in another, 'de man got foh look after he interest to. Ah mean dat is whey he money does come from.'

Rosita dried her hands and went to answer the front door. Oscar occupied the berbice chair, a novel in hand, his pipe smoking, and from the way his legs rested peacefully on the chair's supports, Rosita knew only a fire would budge him.

'It's Serwall,' she called.

'Come on in,' invited Oscar.

'Hi. Hope I'm not interrupting anything.'

'No, have a seat. Don't tell me you're seeing ghosts already.'

'No, no. I'm looking for Lily. She has this knack of disappearing.'

'Relax. Nobody's going to kidnap your daughter, eh, Rosita?' Oscar winked up at her.

'Mr Serwall has every right to be fussy. Lily's a darling.'

'Don't worry with him, ma'am, he'd behave worse if he had a child of his own.'

'Yes, probably,' she replied, and using the dirty dishes as an excuse, vacated the hall. Serwall caught himself.

'I – I'm sorry; I shouldn't have said that.'

'It's nothing,' Oscar promised.

'I really hope she's not ...'

'Not at all. You know, I wouldn't be surprised if Lily went to pay her respects at the bungalow. She's fond of Ben.'

The blood of pride suffused Serwall's cheeks. In spite of the harsh discipline he meted out to Lily, Serwall worshipped the dirt she walked on. She was evidence of his class. It was believed by those who knew Serwall that one error by Lily, social, grammatical, or otherwise, and Serwall was dead.

Oscar puffed gently as he observed the man's bloated manner. Suddenly Serwall picked up the novel and flicked through the pages.

'Good book!'

'Like it?' Oscar was annoyed. There wasn't anything Serwall hadn't read – if he saw you with it first!

'You know,' Serwall avoided the pitfall, 'I've read so many West Indian novels, it isn't funny.'

'Didn't you find this one amusing?'

'Hmm, can't say I remember the story.'

The stories, you imposter! Oscar wanted to retaliate. To add absurdity to error, a book pregnant with satire was bound to titillate the memory. He winced when Serwall plopped the book down, twisting the cover.

Then, rather curiously, Serwall said, 'What's Ben going to do now?'

'Meaning?'

'Well, the diamond business must continue.'

'I don't follow.'

'Well, I'm not ignorant of diamonds myself, so I've been thinking, you know, Ben isn't active and all that, how will he cope?'

'Throughout history,' said Oscar, somewhat coldly, 'polio victims have dealt with the various problems of life. How do you suppose they managed?'

'True, true. But this is different. In Ben's case surely there must be mobility.'

If Serwall had gone on to suggest that he run the show, and let Ben have a percentage of the profits as a silent partner, it might have been easier for Oscar to accept, but the lingering silence, and the anxiety and greed that gleamed in Serwall's eyes made the atmosphere heavy and oppressive. Oscar had been warned about Serwall's appetite for prestige, and the East Indian man's craving for wealth and success was no secret. For Serwall, the lucrative diamond concern seemed almost within his grasp.

For a brief moment there was a look in Oscar's eyes which hinted at something nasty, yet his voice sounded calm when he said, 'Oh, I don't know. In any case I can't see "mobility" being that essential. Ben's situation is unique in that diamond buyers would be prepared to travel up to Mahdia. Let's face it, we aren't exactly behind God's back.'

Serwall frowned. He had overlooked this – his own maxim about the prophet Mohamet and the mountain. Automatically he began to massage the mole near his nose. This was his habit when anything disturbed him. Oscar was repelled by the exercise.

'You have a point,' said Serwall, and he reached down and removed a blade of grass from his shoelace. Then without warning he got up, and offered his hand. Oscar couldn't help reflecting that a minute ago the very fingers in his hand were twirling a repulsive bit of flesh. He glanced to make sure the mole was still in place.

'What about that bottle of XM I have at home?' Serwall tried, sensing the conversation had run sour.

Oscar patted his stomach. 'Never had worms to preserve.'

Making one last, desperate effort at reconciliation, Serwall professed his loyalty to Ben, but declared that, in the event of offering assistance, his hands were tied.

'I doubt Ben'll accept help from anyone.' Oscar stretched the last word, and Serwall felt the acid of sarcasm trickle down his spine. Silently he cursed himself for opening his mouth and left in a haste designed to work off steam.

'Who would believe that was the man who swore to give Ben every support,' said Rosita, who had overheard everything. Oscar closed the door quietly, insisting it was 'one hellofa world.'

Lily was standing before a wall mirror, combing her hair when Serwall burst in. She glanced up nervously.

'Where the devil were you?'

'I – I was watching some boys by the creek,' she lied, 'they caught a camoudi.'

'Boys? What boys?'

'There was So – Somir, Sam ...'

'Listen!' he snapped. 'I don't want you mixing with those damn good-for-nothings! You know I went looking all over the blinking place for you? Make this the last time you give me cause ... Understand?'

'I – I didn't hurry because I – I thought you said you were going to see Mr Tho ...'

At this Serwall lost control.

'I do what the hell I like, but you!' he shook a finger ominously, 'you make sure you don't leave this house without my permission – ever!'

Lily bowed her head but kept an eye on him while he unlaced his shoes furiously. Oscar's cool had dealt him a stinging blow. God Almighty knew it, one day, he'd show Mr High-and-Mighty Thorne a thing or two! Just because his skin was white, because he read a few books, the man thought he was some blasted intellectual! What certificates did he have, anyway? He, Serwall, was a qualified schoolmaster. Just who the hell was Oscar Thorne? Any ass could win the football pools!

Twisting his shoes in his hand, he made for his room when he spotted the fray in the carpet.

'Look, here, girl! Get this blooming thing mended! You're nothing like your mother, rest her soul. Idle, watching snakes – that's what you're fit for! Have you started Pythagoras yet?'

Lily busied herself with the sewing implements. The ends of the green ribbon in her hair fell loosely over her small shoulder when she pulled the carpet into her lap. She'd do her geometry in the morning. She didn't mind darning for it meant peace to think, and she wanted desperately to reflect on the stolen moments near the creek, near the gurgling, icy water. She wondered how her father would have reacted to knowledge of her true whereabouts. The story about the anaconda was days old: she had been with Danny Thorne. When the needle entered the carpet, the fur touched her hand, opening gates of love. Happy, innocent thoughts flooded her mind. Poor Danny, the mosquitoes nearly ate him alive. She stifled a laugh when she remembered how he had been slapping at his neck and back simultaneously while she herself did some on-the-spot marching. Then that rude frog nearly frightened her out of her skin!

That night it rained. The iguana with its soft, flexuous scales, crawled sinuously along the grass, while the labaria eased itself under fallen leaves and waited, and Horatio lifted his head and howled pitifully under the poor shelter offered by an abandoned dray.

2

Rattling and banging as though its bolts would fly out, a lorry raced along the narrow, treacherous track popping stones down a shrub-laden precipice. At times, the vehicle was forced to a crawl to squeeze past giant boulders; sometimes it took fierce thumpings from overhead branches or twigs; sometimes the old tarpaulin covering vital stores flapped deafeningly in the rear. The lone crow circling high above might have wondered whether that little machine progressing at a snail's pace, now disappearing under foliage, now reappearing round a bend, would ever reach its destination.

One hundred and eleven hazardous miles from the mining town of Bartica stood the village of Mahdia, and the only hint of civilisation along this rough, never-ending journey, was the magnificent white, cable-suspension bridge over the Garraway stream.

Years ago, this was impenetrable forest, with lianas frustrating every path, with death lurking everywhere. Prodigious beauty blended with unrefined treachery. In the wee hours of the morning an enchanting mist would mingle with the bewitching aura of aromatic herbs and, with the strong odour of damp earth, the subdued, mysterious wood-noises, the fragrance of wild orchids, cast a spell on all who ventured there. Thousands of birds, some like flying mother-of-pearls, soared over the trees, while monkeys chattered away excitedly, or leapt playfully to and from slender limbs. Monkeys by the score, fascinating with all their little peculiarities.

Gigantic trees with thick, mossed barks, blotted out the sun, zealously concealing their abundant flora and fauna as if from some celestial inquisition – until the gold-seekers arrived. Every foot had to tread warily, however, for this was the hunting ground of the boa constrictor, the jaguar, the labaria, and that colourful but hostile viper, the bushmaster. Tired pork-knockers – even the toughest of prospectors – have made amazing detours to avoid him. In the gay, rushing waters, the piranha were lords. Between fruits, near rocks, in innocent waters, under leaves, terror reigned, and if one slept carelessly in hammocks, small furry, vampire bats were bound to leave a trail of blood.

Hand-sized tarantulas – black, hairy, science-fiction horrors – appeared out of nowhere, and their ability to spring at you was enough to curdle your blood. Scorpions eagerly sought prospectors' boots to convert them into receptacles of comfort. Small wonder that longevity was an unknown word in these regions. Yet, though much of nature was befogged, and sudden death procured little ado, there were numerous consolations.

For the Midas miner, gold nuggets large enough to stagger any imagination, compensated for the perils. For the lover the nature, the exotic flora was breathtaking, and the musical Wren's pre-dawn melody sublime. Butterflies, living rainbows, flitted about aimlessly, and here and there dragonflies – natural baby helicopters, with wings as crisp as cellophane – caused the hungry jaws of lizards to water. The rustling of leaves as racoons and bush-fowls started from the undergrowth in fear, never failed to upset that hollow silence familiar to those who have long dwelled within the limits of a forest.

Sometimes, through a glade, one glimpsed the darting form of a painted leopard as it closed in on its flagging quarry. This indeed was the adventurer's mecca. Always there was activity. If the salamanders didn't take to heel at sudden noises, nature kept constant the presence of life as dead branches crashed through the trees during the quiet of day, a sound sure to startle anyone. There were times when even the silence spoke.

As is usually the case with forests, the frogs chased the flies, the snakes chased the frogs, the mongooses chased the snakes – if they could – and the land was a happy place.

Many years ago, at a clearing in this forest, a pork-knocker arrived. He had faced afflictions and ailments ranging from wasp stings to snake bites, corns to malaria, and was reduced to a walking skeleton. No amount of labba or creek water could have invigorated his despairing soul. His eyes, set deep within two cavernous openings, glinted like steel in the afternoon sun, and his flat, broad nostrils flared with each laboured breath. Those very eyes that had gaped hopefully at every gilded pebble had become slits hiding flames of wrath, and the animal instincts within had risen to frightening proportions.

Miraculously, this wretched soul awoke the next morning to discover that beneath his calloused feet lay what was to become the most coveted El Dorado in all British Guiana. He even found diamonds! Heartened by this windfall the man clapped his hands, danced in glee, and congratulated himself boisterously. He even winked at the scavenger birds that, days before, had had their eyes riveted on him.

As it always happens so enigmatically in the forest, word travelled. Gold! Someone had struck gold! Soon a second pork-knocker showed up, and a second shack rose. Then a third, and before anyone realised it … a village was born.

Unlike many villages, Mahdia became a landmark on the map, achieving economic success in its maturity. Today the gold dredge in the Potaro district no longer reaps its harvest, but its performance can hardly be equalled.

In this region, decades later, Charles Savory gained the position of diamond and gold dealer, and fortune followed him like a shadow from his first transaction. He was loved by the villagers, and trusted by the hard-headed, leather-skinned pork-knockers who sold him their finds – a rare accomplishment. It was said he never refused a beggar. Then, one night, a shot rang out, shattering the silence, and the industrious Charles breathed his last. Ben Savory had long been on tranquillizers for his insomnia and was, therefore, in no position to give a reliable account of what happened. Hypothesis, then, presented this as a probably story.

Charles had vowed to slay an ocelot which had been destroying poultry and small-stock like the plague.

Perhaps the animal – having disturbed Charles that night – made good its escape before he could let fly a single charge and he, frustrated enough to forget the hammers were cocked, dashed down the weapon. At that range the Grand Prix SSG all but carried his throat away.

After the event, every inhabitant perched on a branch of interest wondered: could Ben, a cripple, continue the good work? The question was stamped on every concerned face, and where diamonds were involved, everyone was concerned.

As if he had anticipated these whispers and beckonings, Ben exercised a composure contrary to his short temper, but his paraplegia was reflected in every pair of eyes that regarded him sympathetically. His brother's death proved the turning point in his own life. He swore he would show them that one Savory was as good as another – cripple or no cripple!

It was hot the morning Oscar visited the bungalow. Ben sat on the verandah, in the wheelchair, watching Jim at work. His handyman squatted low while he prepared a stem for tongue-grafting with the type of dexterity one would associate with heart surgery.

The semi-circular flower bed, Jim's obvious delight, bore such red, saucer-sized hibiscus that admirers insisted they would drip blood. Below the hedge, in triangular formation, ran two adorable white and pink periwinkle creepers. Greenheart lined the forest's edge. You could rest assured if you looked at Jim's floricultural achievements and said, 'Jim, dis is de bes garden in de whole world!' someone would run to fetch a doctor when Jim's face started to purple.

Oscar and Ben shook hands and exchanged aimless talk for a while. Oscar's mind had been set, but now, in Ben's presence, the old indecision swept over him. He dug at a speck of paint on the balustrade.

'Ben, do you mind if I – I enquired about the business?'

The cripple merely shifted, but it were as if the sounds in the village had suddenly died of fright. His eyes, lined pink by a series of wide morning yawns, blinked undecidedly.

'Listen, Oscar, you're the one man I like around here, really, but let's understand each other. I'm easily riled when people throw that "poor-old-soul" stuff at me; I can't stand it!'

'I don't intend to fling any poor-old-soul stuff at you. Besides, I don't care if you get upset; this is important.'

Ben made to dismiss the topic with a wave of the hand, but hesitated.

'Look you know why I didn't keep a wake. You know I despise gossip! I can't stand crocodile tears. What's the difference if I get a pat from people who don't give a shit if I eat tomorrow?'

'I know, I know,' Oscar cut in. 'But try to understand the position of Mahdia ... of Fieldor. He has to eat, too! You must get things in their proper perspective. These people are inquisitive, yes, but that's a harmless weakness. Believe me, most of them mean well. Anyway, you have to realise if you don't buy the diamonds, you wouldn't earn a cent, and whatever Charles left will quickly expire.' Oscar brushed a fly from his nose. 'Unless the pork-knockers get your cash, Fieldor won't get paid for his supplies. The pork-knockers need you, Fieldor needs the pork-knockers, and you need the diamonds. People need people, Ben.'

Ben breathed hard, and the wens of his wide jaws dilated rapidly. Oscar couldn't help noticing how the muscles on the man's forearms stood out like old vines.

'All right!' Ben heaved, 'all right, let's just say you're right ...' He peered up at Oscar. 'Why me? Why would the pork-knockers do business with me? There's no contract. They owe me nothing! I'm a cripple, Oscar. I – I can't get out of this blasted chair!'

'Hold it! That's no issue! Look, there's no one in Mahdia with your knowledge of gold, or diamonds. Many claim you were better than Charles; that you could spot a "sweet-man" under water.'

'All right, even so ...' He turned away agitatedly. 'What then? The pork-knockers get their money and pay Fieldor, but what about the diamonds? I can't eat them. Who can I trust to negotiate for me? They'd run off with everything. Diamonds are a serious business.'

Oscar leaned forward. 'No, silly. All you do is write to the agent in Georgetown, let him travel up to Mahdia once every couple of months or so....'

'What?' Ben expostulated. 'Who in his right senses would want to travel ...?'

'For *diamonds*! you must be crazy!' Oscar looked at him in total disbelief. He pulled out a white handkerchief, wiped his face, and continued to shake his head incredulously.

Ben's expression went blank. An avalanche of doubt buried him. He heard Oscar's voice.

'The agent needs your diamonds much as you need his money. It's his livelihood. Look, give it a try. Draft the man a letter. Make him an offer worth his sweat.'

Oscar wiped his brow again, and stuffed the hanky into his trouser pocket.

Slowly, Ben looked up at him, and for a moment it seemed he would say, 'You're okay,' but the words never came. He sighed. 'All right, I'll write to the damn guy!'

In spite of the fresh beads of perspiration on his forehead, Oscar smiled. He knew one injudicious remark could have sparked off an emotional outburst, for Ben – courageous though he was – had a tendency to lean on nostalgia. Better still, Ben had conquered his pride in this simple concession. He laughed, and Ben joined in, as if at some familiar joke. Even Jim, whose hearing was suspect, squinted up at them in wonder.

Sam and Somir came to blows. They had been gambling under the flamboyant tree in Oscar's back yard. Somir was cuffing the daylights out of Sam when the latter tripped, and fell. Across the open ground Oscar saw Sam lying propped up by the elbows. Somir was standing astride him, fists clenched.

Oscar sucked his teeth. 'I'll settle that boy's ass!' he said, and was transformed into a living bulldozer. It wasn't for want of scolding, or threatening, that Somir enticed younger boys into the gamblimg mechanism. No matter who shook a cautioning finger, or upbraided him, Somir shrugged it off. Oscar charged toward them with surprising speed for his years, but his left shoe landed in a pool of water and started to squelch frightfully.

Danny's reverie was broken by the noise. Somir! His pulse-beat quickened. He ran outside, demanding, 'What's the meaning of this in our yard?' But whatever thoughts he entertained of tongue-lashing Somir, fate had decreed otherwise. For his bravery, he received a scratch when Somir made to slap him and missed.

Oscar had entered the gate, his shirt billowing, his hair blowing, his shoe sounding the advance like a rebellious frog. This sound alerted Somir, and before anyone could gather their wits, he was up and over the high corrugated zinc fence like a stray cat in inglorious flight.

Panting, his wide shoulders heaving, his stomach swelling against his shirt, Oscar turned upon Sam. Then he noticed the blood on Danny's forehead. His lips puckered in fury. God! The innocent always pay! He pulled Danny to him, placing a hand behind the boy's neck. Danny, who till now had said nothing, cried.

'Why?' Oscar looked at Sam, 'Why do you follow that – that …' Here he extended a palm as though he expected Sam to wrap up an explanation and hand it over.

Sam eyed the hand while he nursed the throbbing spot near his temple. He was in no mood to relate episodes. Besides, his shirt, stuck fast to his back, made him feel irritable.

'Very well,' said Oscar, stuffing his shirt in his trousers, 'but make this the last time you disgrace this yard!' Sam avoided those piercing eyes. 'As for that no-good Somir, I'll wring his blessed neck! I'll tear out his liver! I'll …!'

'Oscar!' cried Rosita, appearing on the step, her arms folded. She seemed rather amused by her husband's unkempt hair and soaked shoe. Sam sighed in relief at Mrs Thorne's presence, and when Oscar and Danny began to explain what had happened, it gave him the chance to slip quietly away. Sweat poured down his temples and nose, and the look in his eyes hinted at hell's fire.

'Let's go put something on that forehead,' said Oscar, guiding Danny up the steps.

'Why does he do it?' Danny asked.

'What, son?'

'Somir, I mean; why does he go about playing the bully?'

Oscar pushed his hair into place with his fingers set like a four-pronged comb, and a lock fell over his forehead.

'I'm afraid you don't understand, son.'

'What?'

'Well, Somir has a reason for hating everyone. You in particular.

'Me? Why?'

'Just take my word for it. One reason is jealousy. His father's a dipsomaniac, and he hasn't got a mother. Maybe, it's not his fault. All I ask for the present is that you forgive and forget. Believe me, he'll come to nought.'

Oscar had swallowed his anger and, indeed, his calm had returned. He studied his finger nails like a philosopher.

'No, we shouldn't be harsh on him.'

Not long afterwards, Tiny, the milkman, made his rounds. His bell rang non-stop while a horde of children marched behind him pretending at soldiers. When Tiny ignored them, they produced margarine-tin drums, old saucepans and bottles, and beat upon them with sticks and iron rods. The sounds of their inglorious orchestras never failed to excite fits of laughter. Their drums, more like pans tumbling down stairs, caused mothers to cover their mouths, stifling shrieks of merriment. The pot-bellied, hot-tempered dairyman was so small, his big-frame bicycle leaned upon him like the gates of Gaza and it screeched monstrously.

It seemed he would collapse under the weight of those huge milk-cans, but every day, without fail, he appeared, and shuffled from house to house to distribute his milk to grateful customers.

Sometimes the children were overbearing. He would stop and glare at them, and immediately the procession would come to a bumping halt. Sometimes he shooed them away in total disgust, then the mob would gesture back, like royalty fanning manicured nails to the wind, and cry, 'Oh, shoo yourself, Tiny!' At this, he would almost drop his bike to shake a terrible fist at them, and when he cursed, the children dropped all pretence, stuck out sweet-stained tongues, some red, some purple, and struck up their popular song:

'Ting-a-ling-a-ling, Tiny coming,
Ting-a-ling-a-ling, wid he milk spilling,
Ting-a-ling-a-ling, wid he belly swinging,
Ting-a-ling-a-ling, wid he beatty haul in.'

Danny, prostrate on the floor, sniggered as he listened to the chorus. Tiny complained at every house, and mothers, particularly those of the culprit children, sympathised genuinely, but whenever they heard the tune, even they couldn't resist humming 'Ting-a-ling-a-ling' for it had that lively beat.

Danny had his nose burined in Oscar's *Animal Book*, enraptured by the colourful illustration of a boa constrictor wrapped around the frail body of a fawn. There were few sufferings this book couldn't mitigate, and it proved a constant eraser for the many thoughts of his disorientation in the lonely village. Since their arrival in Mahdia, a sort of silent treaty existed between the other boys and himself. He knew it – they knew it. Yet, he was happy. He loved everything he saw, but above all, he loved her; in her there was life. If only they would let him be! Somir's hatred alone had the contageousness of the plague.

Even as his fingers felt for the wound still fresh on his forehead, his eyes burned, and the book before him merged with two salty teardrops. Oscar had insisted he forget, and he would try, because he respected Oscar's prudence, but he knew it wasn't going to be easy.

Sam burned with hate. The hell with Somir! Forgive? Sam mistrusted the word. Besides, forgiveness travelled with dignity, chivalrous knights in shining armour, and all the other crap they used to read in school! Since Sam had heard about *lex talionis* from a pork-knocker, that was that! Weren't these violent times? Yes! And no Gita nor bible was going to make a sissy out of him!

He hurried home, snapped his head under a pipe, and unchained Rex. Instantly, the alsatian reared to greet him, and Sam went staggering under its weight. Rex bathed Sam's face with uncontrolled passions while his big tail sent pebbles flying in every direction.

'Down, boy, down!' implored Sam, struggling to maintain his balance. 'Somir is the same one who does pelt you, Rex, he is the louse!' He stroked the golden mane until Rex calmed appreciably. Somir – the thief!

He guessed that Somir would venture down to the creek after two o'clock for a swim. When the heat was terrific Somir spent long hours in the water. Well, the sun was up, and Sam vowed, he would be waiting!

Few children were playing on the dusty road when he crept out of the yard with Rex on a leash. Far in the east, rain clouds had gathered menacingly over a green sea that was the forest; in the distance they rested like gigantic grey boulders. Above, two carrion crows circled leisurely.

The two disappeared into a secret path in the forest where strong light-beams pierced the leaves, and insects chirped in subdued tones. A quick inspection told Sam they were alone. Healthy spittle dripped from Rex's jaws. Finally they arrived at vantage point near a clearing by the creek. In a state of excitement Sam dropped to his knees, and parted the bushes. His entire body flashed hot and cold when he saw Somir and, of a sudden, a bitter hatred filled his heart. Imagine – his own race taking advantage of him! He thought about those history cases where an Indian son would do his own mother out of a property, or where brothers cut one another's throats for bigger shares immediately the parents' eyes were closed. Silently Sam conceded that sometimes he was ashamed of his own people.

At Somir's playful voice, Rex's ears flicked up, and his hackles rose. Even among the noise and indelible odour of buckbead and sage, Rex picked up the scent and voice of a foe. Two fang teeth accompanied a low growl. Sam undid the leash. Rex shot from the thicket, ears pasted back, tail sweeping the grass. He had not forgotten this lad. Once,

Rex had torn his nose through the paling trying to reach the outside enemy with the stones.

Somir, shouting and sparring at the rushing waters, stood naked on the bank pretending to be a champion wrestler who kicked back his opponents fast as they crawled up. Perhaps, it was the sudden lull that fell over the creek that caused him to turn his head. Whatever the warning, Somir's eyes nearly popped at the sight of the golden form flying at him. He swallowed litres when he dived screaming into the creek, but was soon scrambling up the opposite bank like a drenched monkey in panic.

Then the realisation dawned upon Sam – the monstrosity of his premeditation! If Rex had caught Somir, the result could have been disastrous. He felt actual relief at Somir's safety. The water was so icy, even Rex avoided it, but his instincts served him well. He looked around, scratched himself a comfortable bed, and reposed in the warm sand. Somir stood trembling on the bank opposite; Sam could even see the goose-bumps on his skinny legs! Somir's fate hung like the drop of water on his nose.

Sam chuckled. He knew what it was like to be naked out there! Once in the water you were safe, but outside! With the wind pressing! The silvery water shimmered as the breeze crept northward, parting the reeds, penetrating into Somir's bones. The rain clouds had edged nearer, darkening the sun, adding to Somir's plight.

But for marabuntas, Somir would never have guessed Sam's presence, or that his dilemma was no accident. Sam upset a nest, and the reddish fiends went on the rampage. Bawling, and slapping madly at invisible assailants, he emerged from the bushes; Somir could only look on with his mouth wide open. But the biting cold quickly restored him to his predicament.

'Sam? Ow, Sam, is you, bay?' He cupped his hands. 'Ow, bay, I didn't mean foh tek you money; ah really sarry. For true, bay, ow, call aff you dag, noh?'

Sam advanced nonchalantly and reclined near Rex, his face set. 'You lying! You only saying so foh now?'

'Sam,' Somir tilted his head in a mercy plea, 'Ah swear,

look, ah swear. Ah really sarry; look, ah kneeling down.'

Indeed, Somir was on his knees, his hands reverently clasped. He looked like a compassionate yogi meditating in the nude. Suddenly Sam was angry with himself. He knew, somehow, he would pardon Somir. He couldn't say why, but that was how it had always been. Yet, hurt that Somir had cuffed him, he pretended to be giving the matter grave consideration.

Somir never let up. 'Sam, foh true, wazn't you I did wan foh hit, waz dat black dag, Danny. He wuz de wan dat should'a get dis.' He displayed a clenched fist, the weapon he would have used to demolish Danny. These words stirred the silent enemy. Presently Sam became quite amiable.

Somir grinned foolishly as he slipped on his clothes, but had it not been for Rex, he would have dealt the unsuspecting Sam the blow of the century! Shivering, he took off, leaving Sam feeling like Alexander the Great.

That morning, after feeding his chicken, Danny headed in the direction of the creek. He took the track Sam had used the previous day. A woodpecker flew past, landed on a nearby tree, and proceeded to hammer away like an angry sheriff nailing up a 'wanted' poster. High above circled a snail hawk.

Had the brute spotted his chicken? he wondered in alarm, unfamiliar with the various species of hawks. But his fears were soon allayed, for out of nowhere, scraps of fruit falling from their beaks, darted two kis-kadees. Like practised aerobats they darted after the carnivore. The hawk hovered shakily, then dived into the trees, only to emerge yelping and dodging with the aggressive birds hot in pursuit. Danny smiled. The piercing war-cries of the kis-kadees shattered the morning's peace as they zeroed in like fighter planes after a helpless freighter.

Danny was about to leave the forest when the soft patter of feet reached his ears. He listened, barely breathing. Fear began to creep up on him, for the forest was extremely quiet. The feet were fast approaching.

'Sam?' he called. No answer. 'Somir?' Still nothing.

The tripping feet sounded perilously close. Danny's heartbeat went wild! Suddenly a form appeared before him, like in a dream.

'Lily!'

'Shh!' Soft lips puckered behind a forefinger. He stared, doubting his eyes; that she was here! The sun had not yet cleared the tree tops.

'Where are you going?'

'To the moon, silly,' then, 'I came to tell you that Dad is going to Bartica tomorrow – I don't know when he'll be back.'

Danny's thoughts weren't coming straight. 'I – I can see you, then?'

'Why do you think I'm here, Danny Thorne?'

'On the hill?'

'Yes. I'll bring along some lemonade, or ginger beer, if you prefer.'

His teeth shone. He bubbled with joy, and his thoughts kept deserting him.

'What time?' His eyes sought hers.

''Bout nine.' She glanced anxiously over his shoulder, then touched his arm. 'I have to run; see you tomorrow:'

He watched as she flitted away on tiptoe: the place where she had touched his arm was alive with the strangest sensations, now warm, now cold. He placed his finger there and was profoundly happy.

A moment ago present, now gone. Why was everything beautiful so temporary? Humming his favourite tune he headed towards the creek, a towel round his neck. Whenever he was happy, or sad, the lyrics of this simple song placed his soul in unison with the event and, somehow, made him whole.

> 'I'll walk a mile,
> with a smile,
> for my momma and pappa....'

That night a gale raced across the village. The leaves of the banana lashed out viciously. Heavy trees swayed and creaked like ancient hinges, branches snapped like twigs, and leaves went eddying and spinning madly in the sudden scuds. Then came the rain.

The wind howled and caterwauled, and trees replied with swishing fury, and, suddenly, a terrific thunderclap silenced the land. But throughout the night forked lightning continued to engrave the frightening patterns in the charcoal sky, and the rumblings persisted like the pounding of hooves in a hippodrome somewhere in the heavenly metropolis.

3

Serwall scribbled in his diary in the light of the kerosene lamp. A pair of trousers, coloured chalk; things he required for himself he listed under 'his', those for Lily under 'hers' – dress material, needles, and slippers. Then he wrote alongside: NB – comprehension and maths books. Some students were making rapid progress, but Danny and Lily were miles ahead, and he had to concentrate on them. Then he considered buying Lily a wristwatch. After all, Oscar had presented Danny with an expensive one – a child not of his own blood. He, Serwall, must give Lily the best! These peasants missed nothing! Besides, Lily had attained puberty, beginning to mould like her mother.

On his desk stood a picture of Sati. They had been married for ten years when late in December, four years ago, she fell ill, and died a month later.

'Leukaemia, Mr Serwall, nothing we can do,' said the doctor. Four years ago, yet it seemed like four weeks. He looked closely at the photograph, at the eyes of the woman whose unselfish love had knitted their marriage in spite of his wretched moods, and something within him shifted. He had never realised how much she meant to him. She was ever present, yet unobtrusive. She – he discovered soon after the funeral – had been his source of inspiration, his mainstay. With her unquestionable loyalty, she had made him a teacher of all teachers. Her silent adoration, her unconcealed amazement – as he scribbled away on the blackboard, as the chalk diminished and the mathematical equation on the board developed into frightening proportions – made him a genius. Not that he was not – well, a brilliant man – it was just that he – he needed her. He sat quietly, remembering her devotion, her humility, and the weight of his affliction was merciless.

He closed the diary, pocketed the pen, and leaned back,

tilting the chair. It creaked, and the eyes in the photograph seemed to look up at him in troubled concern. He brought the chair to rest squarely on the floor for he knew she would have cautioned, 'Watch how you're leaning, dear.' Strange, he never once returned that concern; he accepted it as a tribute to his status. 'Foolish man!' he soliloquised, and in a few moments of grief, bowed his head, and wept.

Lily was tidying her room when he approached, he stood at the door, a silhouette against the light in the hall.

'You'll be sleeping when I leave in the morning. Don't forget to lock the door if you go out. Walk with your key, too; you don't want to get locked out. And don't forget your manners. A good-morning or good-afternoon takes nothing off you.'

'Yes, daddy.'

Saturday meant no school, but for Danny it meant something special. Today he would be with her. He made his bed, and set about with towel and soap. He filled a bucket from the large wooden tub – the one that accumulated moss – and washed on the back steps, dipping the cold water with a calabash.

Inside, the cuckoo clock cuckooed six times. The village was dark, and all around the trees in a veil of mist were grey, sleeping monsters. He soaped vigorously, but couldn't keep off the goose pimples. He felt like imitating Oscar by burring aloud, but didn't wish to wake Rosita.

While he dried, he recited extracts from *Romeo and Juliet*. Last night he had planned everything with such accuracy, Sherlock Holmes would have been dumbfounded. He would breakfast at seven, dress by eight, brush his teeth at a quarter past then, until a quarter to nine, he would peruse over the lines he had ticked, to keep them fresh in his mind. Then a brisk walk up the hill and he should find Lily anxiously waiting for him.

Pleased at his precision, he picked up a hand mirror and contemplated his face. Two pin-hole dimples were activated by his smile – boy, wasn't he proud of them!

However, as is often the problem with boys his age,

Danny's meticulous schedule got entangled with his emotions. What if he arrived late and found her gone? This question haunted him. Consequently, he left the house at seven – without breakfast – to keep his nine o'clock rendezvous, and sat on the hill, a small version of 'The Thinker', until Lily arrived.

He felt like that self-conscious gentleman, who, strolling with his head high, thinking about his expensive attire and good looks, had heard a charming woman remark – to the accompaniment of an embarrassing snigger – 'your fly's open, mister!'

Danny whistled low when he saw her. Not that she wore crepe de chine, or chiffon, or anything lustrous, or that she used mascara, or eyebrow pencil; her delicate, natural beauty did the trick. Danny agreed the name Lily had never been used more accurately.

His legs outstretched on the dry, stubbled grass, his fingers squeezing the dark stem of a cactus, he contemplated her with eyes of love. A drop of liquid pulped, and trickled down his hand.

'Been waiting long?' She set down the basket.

'No.'

'That's going to stain!' she warned as the chlorophyll dropped near his pants. 'You men!'

'What?'

'I bet if you had to wash your clothes, you wouldn't be messing about with stainy things!'

'Sorry,' he offered, and wanted to add how exciting she looked when she scolded him, as Oscar often told Rosita.

She folded a cloth and sat down, inviting him to join her. A few red ants crawled about the grass. Two blue-sackies, one close on the other's tail, went past in two dips.

'Smells good!' he said, beckoning to the basket.

'It should,' she jested, 'I swamped it with essence.'

Danny sat back happy and relaxed; then came her unexpected, 'Isn't it true that most West Indian men, after working their wives to death, causing them to become misshapen, or fat, sneak away to seek "consolation" from their friends over a bottle? Or go chasing after some fly-by-night chick?'

'I – I don't know … but not me! I'll take good care of – of … well, whoever I marry.' For him, 'taking care' meant placing a blanket up to the wife's neck, kissing her forehead, feeding her broth and telling her 'wicked' things. He knew nothing beyond this, but Rosita often said that Oscar was 'horrible' or 'wicked' after he had whispered something to her. Danny always pretended that he hadn't heard. The whispered things must be all right, however, for Rosita always seemed to like them, whatever she said. He flushed at the thought of such rebukes from Lily.

Under the alert sun the trees cast long, dark shadows, and everywhere quietude prevailed. Danny felt there was enough silence here for a god. In the valley the greenery shifted lazily, and fragile ferns quivered on the hillside. They sat in the shade of a sawari, watching spots of sunlight become animated all around. Where he had previously wiped his hands, many crushed blades of grass began to flick upwards like weak but stubborn signals on a cardiograph.

'Are you a Christian?'

'Yes.' He shifted uncomfortably. 'Why?'

'Do you know I'm a Hindu?' She arranged slices of pone and sponge in a serviette.

'What's the difference?' He accepted the napkin with a frown.

'Oh, I don't know. It's just that – that parents are so touchy when it comes to their daughter, or – or son, marrying into a different religion.' She shrugged matter-of-factly, then handed him a glass. 'Hope the swank isn't too sour.'

Danny felt the urge to say 'Hindu, Juju, Baboo – what's the fuss,' but thought against it. He pondered.

'You don't mean your dad would object if we wanted to marry?'

'We? Marry? Are you proposing?'

'Well, I – I mean if – if you had agreed. …'

His embarrassment made her titter, and her face reflected great happiness.

'But seriously, Lily, wouldn't he consent?'

'Why should he?'

'Why should he?' cried Danny in near exasperation. 'He – he knows me! He knows us, dad, and mom, and me! We're family friends!'

'But you're not a Hindu,' she persisted, pouring herself a drink. 'Here, have another tissue, your dimples are too deep. Anyway, you don't really know my father.' She herself couldn't fathom why religion was that important when people were in love. Surely God was love!

He sipped his lemonade, then returned to the battle.

'What is it about being a Hindu? Christ died for the world! He shed His blood for everyone. There is only *one* Saviour. No other person, or religion, can be of much consequence.'

'Is that so?' But Lily seemed rather curious about this Jesus. 'Have you ever heard of Lord Krishna, or Lord Rama?'

'Lord who?'

'Rama.'

'No.'

'Well, how can you tell, then?'

He couldn't. 'Tell you what,' he stammered. 'we'll both do some homework; later we'll compare notes. How's that?'

'Fine.'

'I hope I'm right, Lily,' he said, and prayed she detected the tenderness in his 'Lily'. She must have, for she glanced up briefly and her eyes reflected the affection in her heart. His pulse went racing! She was beautiful – too beautiful! If only he were handsome! Waves of frustration tossed him about.

'Have you ever felt afraid, Danny,' she asked.

'Afraid? What of?' but immediately he recalled how he felt when Somir had challenged him to a fight.

'I'm not sure. Maybe I'm being silly, but sometimes I have this – this feeling that something awful will happen to me.'

'You mean … dreams?' He thought of Rosita, and how Oscar constantly fretted about her 'infernal dreams', the interpretations of which always left Oscar with some 'mysterious' lover.

'No, not dreams, just a feeling. At times I'm really scared.' Danny cleared his throat. Was she trying to frighten him? Was she as terrified of this something as he was of Somir? He looked up, but no, she had not been reading his mind. Funny, he reflected, how people feared for their innermost thoughts; even a chance look in their direction sufficed to activate their pendulum of suspicion.

Oscar had said that the human coffer was vulnerable; not only were the secrets of relatives insecure, but also one's own treasured thoughts, for often they were found scrawled on the walls of iniquity, or penned in the scrolls of truth. For a long while, neither attempted to upset the silence that had become sacred.

Far beyond the untamed, eye-soothing verdure of forest, far up and across the rugged mountains, a cloud collided with a summit. Danny contemplated nature's fray and in a flash memories came rushing back. *Quo Vadis* – a film shown to the orphans many years ago. Vividly he remembered the battle between Ursus – a guardian – and a black bison. The scene he detested most – Nero stroking his goatee in sadistic delight, while the jewels on his fingers – incandescent things, manifestations of paganism – reflected the evil in his heart. Yet that barbaric soul was to be disappointed, for the sweating, blood-smeared Ursus, with a prodigious effort, twisted and snapped the bull's neck! Thousands of spectators rose to their feet, cheering madly. Then pandemonium broke loose! Nero had gripped the arms of his throne like a man brutally stabbed in the back.

Danny had counted the giant's success as a personal triumph – a victory for the underdog, his tears had brimmed over. That the infamous King fled from the amphitheatre only enhanced the suspicion that dictators, megalomaniacs, and the rest, were a pack of cowards!

In his mind's eye he saw countless Christians being thrown to lions, burned at the stake, crucified for their fate – all for the gratification of ruthless Caesars. He wondered how such barbaric nations could be proud;

wondered about man's quest for entertainment and experienced deep-rooted sympathy for those hapless Innocents.

Kings, at least, should have known that there was a limit to worldly pleasures, that once moderation was abandoned, chaos stepped in. Even Oscar – who was no king – knew that the forerunners of permanent horror were those 'experiments' to extract the ultimate in worldly pleasure.

He was deep in thought when Lily climbed to her feet, shook her skirt free of grass, and stepped over to the edge of the hill. Below the valley stretched far and wide. She gazed absently at the trees, the hassocks, the fissures in the face of the opposite hill, the mounds in the valley, and enjoyed the rain-scented wind drifting in from the north. A breeze ruffled her skirt, then lifted it. She clutched down, but not before Danny's alert eye had observed two smooth, light brown legs. Guilt knifed into him, and he turned away quickly.

'I caught you!' she remonstrated, and the blood shot into his face. But she was smiling at him knowingly.

Presently, two white blossoms floated down, touching her hair, and childish fantasies seized him. Snow – something he had seen only in the movies – fell from blue clouds – pink flakes at that – like confetti, touching her head and shoulders, falling at her feet to materialise into pink fairies, each one curtsying elegantly before her. His fantasy would have progressed had not a cow mooed rebelliously, fettering his thoughts

'Scram!' he ordered, barely above a whisper.

'What did you say?'

'You heard me?'

'Of course. What did you say?'

'Nothing, really. I was just thinking.'

'And you always talk to yourself?'

'No, it's just that stupid cow there, mooing like a – a cow.'

She laughed heartily. 'You're silly!' At that moment, with a zephyr fanning her hair, her head thrown back, her eyes closed, her laughter a melody ... Danny's love was

sealed. One stanza, one line, of the verses he had studied –
dear Father! But the memory-activating mechanism was
stuck! Then a force more powerful than he lifted him to
his feet. It compelled him towards Lily, made him turn
her shoulders, and kiss her, if somewhat awkwardly.

It happened so quickly, Danny was staggered by his
own actions. His head reeling, his emotions galloping like
phantom steers, he returned to his seat. He had been
entranced, but he had accomplished a dream! He had
kissed Lily!

In the sky a tiny silver disc grew larger until they could
hear the hum of the cargo plane. Even seated, Danny's
legs trembled.

Lily smiled. Little love bubbles filled her heart. She felt
light, and free! She had often wondered if he would ever
kiss her.

Then it happened. Out of nowhere he appeared, a sneer
twisting his face, his arms flinging. Danny sat up erect, his
jaw set, then he got shakily to his feet, his heart sinking
fast. Somir stood hands akimbo.

'Don't make me brock-up no love scene, yoh hear,' he
drawled, and looked ready to pounce on Danny and tear
off his face. Danny moved over to Lily protectively and
Somir laughed, jealousy clawing away at his breast. Then
he started to hum the popular tune from *Amar*, and clap
his hands. It was difficult to assess his thoughts. He
sauntered down the hill, his voice trailing off in the
wind.

Lily beckoned to Danny, 'Let's go.' Danny's tongue felt
heavy. The hand of fear had gripped the words in his
throat. Whenever Lily spoke he responded only by
shaking his head, one way or the other.

With a rusty nail in his heart, Somir walked home. The
thoughts flowing in his head were soaked in gall. The
whore! Imagine he, Somir, an Indian … like her! Yet she
preferred the company of a nigger! She was less than a
whore! The bitch!

So engrossed in thought was Somir, he failed to notice
an observer not ten metres from the footpath. Slowly the
painted leopard withdrew, and skulked away in the

undergrowth. Somir descended, his mind active. Further down, through a narrow vista, the animal reappeared and stared at Somir with starved, demonic eyes, its soft nostrils dilating rapidly.

On the road Somir halted, and bit upon his thumb, all the while shaking his head in acknowledgement of some brilliant scheme. Lily's unexpected disgrace had shocked him beyond words. And pretending to be all quiet and virtuous; the bitch! He kicked at a tin vengefully. Then he stoned a cow, the missile landing with cruel impact. He grabbed a limb and shook it until, exhausted, he sank to his knees and doubled over in anguish.

Jim was in the garden when it happened. A woman screamed. People were running towards the bungalow. Jim shelved the shears, walked over to the shed, and was about to take out a spade, when a sudden movement behind a condemned coop arrested his attention. Of course, Jim hadn't heard the shouting, nor noticed the approaching crowd gesticulating like lunatics.

He tiptoed, peeped over, and exclaimed, staggering back. On the ground lay a lamb, its stomach open, its entrails scattered like sodden rope. Its once snow-white coat was a study in scarlet. By now Ben's yard was crowded, some armed with axes, others sticks, or cutlasses.

'I see it; I see it!' cried Jim, and questions poured in. How high? How long? How fearsome, a tiger? One man calmly informed them that there were no true tigers in America, and the people denounced him as an 'educated ass,' and advised him to get his facts straight. Some lamented over the destruction of the lamb in such wailing tones, an outsider would have believed elephants had just trampled to death all the children of Mahdia.

'Ben still got he brother gun,' one pork-knocker reminded and a hairy-chested, sleepy-eyed companion cupped his crotch, saying, 'Buddy, dis is de owny gun I gon hold.'

Everybody laughed, except the owners of the lamb.

Lily, on seeing the mangled body, grew afraid. She

edged over to Danny. 'I'm going,' she whispered, and he nodded.

Nothing could be done about Somir's discovery. But did he see them embracing? Danny hoped not. His insides ached; one never took Somir lightly. He looked at the bloody trail across the grass. How many fowls, ducks, and small stock this ocelot had slaughtered, no one knew for sure, but the approximate tally was making people nervous.

One man predicted that the next stage was children, and mothers' knees watered. Poultry rearers began to erect sturdy fences; a few cattle owners even set crude traps – more in the hope of scaring off the killer – but these were so ill-designed, some suggested that a further protective fence be installed, for the children's safety. Those who couldn't afford fences slept at their window-sills.

Danny sauntered off, hands in his pockets, kicking aimlessly at bricks. Kissing Lily had been an indescribable joy. He wondered if her experience equalled his. Had she felt that swelling of the heart, that drowning of the consciousness in a vortex of love? Then he remembered Somir, the scourge of his life!

Mahdia's only parlour – owned and operated by Fieldor – stood near the main road. Danny felt in his fob, and toyed with his shillings. He had enough to buy a bar of chocolate, and marshmallows. He had already eaten, and he knew Rosita would be cross if he picked at her food, so he deliberated, but his sweet-tooth swayed his conscience, and he turned towards the shop.

You can imagine Danny's surprise, when on leaving again, he found six boys waiting outside the shop, some on the incline bridge, some on the road on their haunches. A minute ago the place was deserted! Needles of fear pricked at him. His pockets bulging, he descended the steps uneasily. Then someone pulled at his shoelace.

He turned. 'Did I trouble you, Somir?'

'Did I trouble you, Somir?' Somir mimicked and, turning to the others, 'You bays ever hear such good language, eh? Dis black bay is a real Englishman!'

'Somir,' teased Sam, applying new fire, 'is why you troblin' de poo bay?'

Sam, incidentally, had been given Somir's version of the episode on the hill. Sam's response was, 'I always knew she was nothing!' Ingenuous, gullible, was Sam. Somir had only to breathe the word, and the word was good. Even Sam could not understand why Danny had suddenly become an outcast with woolly hair! That Lily had committed that inconceivable act, well, for Sam it was a bitter reminder that, once, she had smiled with him, such an innocent, warm smile, who would have thought she was a slut?

Somir leaped up, made shivering movements that shammed fear, then scratched his head like a comedian. The others cheered encouragingly. He started to sing:

> 'Black bay moder leave he in de gutter,
> An gone 'way wid ten men,
> Pooo black bay, he ain' gat noobady.'

At the mention of his mother, Danny's lip tightened, but this exhibition only heartened Somir. He continued:

> 'Blah, blah, black sheep,
> 'Ave you any moder,
> No, sah, no, sah,
> Owny twenty fader.'

Tears settled in Danny's eyes. He turned away, but a stone struck him in the back. He winced, and glared at the mob, but fear and anger were blending in his heart.

Somir sprang forward, thumbing his chest, his insides scorching with hate. 'Is I do it, black bay; is I pelt you rass!' Someone hissed, 'Bax he, Somir, bax the f-ing nigger!'

Acid flowed through Danny's veins and he turned, as a kitten would, even if cornered by a fierce dobermann.

'Fight, Danny, fight!' urged a silent voice, 'for your mother's honour!'

Somir didn't expect Danny's show of aggression. It was only a push, but it was sudden, vicious, and all Danny really knew about the martial arts. Somir went crashing into the boys behind.

Sam rubbed his hands in glee. 'Wha, Danny fighting back?'

Somir composed himself, and circled Danny, a tower of confidence. Seeing the uncertainty, even apology, in Danny's eyes, he lunged forward. Rigid of limb, Danny held his ground. Somir struck like lightning. Two left jabs caught Danny on the forehead. Anyone could have seen that Somir's indomitability matched Danny's indecision.

Feinting a blow, Somir caught him off guard, and fired a hard right that struck the immobile Danny plumb in the chest. He staggered, wincing, only to receive a rough push from hostile hands behind. Thrown upon his enemy, Danny struck out in desperation, catching Somir a wild slap across the ear, but this merely enriched the bully's fury. Somir retaliated with a swinging uppercut that connected with Danny's chin. He cried out as a fist landed in his back. Now everyone was throwing a punch! Someone shrieked, 'Ow, you-all don' kill de lil' blackie!'

Finally, they drew blood. Danny clutched at his belly. Tears were bathing his face, his body was on fire, and still they kept pounding him! Somir had vowed to teach this black bitch a lesson! After a while, the hurt penetrated to Danny's heart.

The chocolate was putty in his pocket, and his marshmallows were foaming out. Shocks of pain exploded everywhere. He never dreamed fighting could be like this. When they threw him on the ground the pebbles claimed his skin and his hip looked as if wasps had been at it. The red dust powdered his hair, and blood trickled everywhere.

Fortunately for the brigands, Fieldor had retired to the rear of the parlour, but Lloyd, a thickset bow-legged pork-knocker, rescued Danny. He scattered the lot with one sweep of his broad hand. Somir landed on his rear, and Sam went tumbling in the grass. The others fled. Danny was escorted home; sniffing, his face contorted, his legs trembling, he looked a pitiful sight.

Oscar raved. He decried Somir's tyranny, his hands

shooting about like a sea-scout sending out distress signals, and for the hundredth time he swore to 'fix Somir's ass, once and for all.'

Lloyd shook his head doubtfully. After all, he, Oscar, was white. How could he know what it felt like to be black? To hear the insult 'black dogs', was one thing, to be the black dog, another.

Lloyd had heard the boys calling Danny a 'nigger bastard', and it cut into him, for he realised that that was exactly how others would label his illegitimate sons in Bartica. A week later, unbeknown to anyone, Lloyd visited Bartica and secretly married his common-law wife.

Rosita wrung her hands, grimaced at the blood, and went so pale, Oscar had to pat her head with spirits after bathing Danny's wounds.

Broken-hearted, Danny retired to his room, and locked himself in. Never before had he felt this terrible urge to be alone. To think. Why? Why was he different? What corruption had he brought to Mahdia? Why was he despicable in their eyes? Was he evil? What? Why? God! From the awful wilderness called grief he sought to escape, but the words 'nigger bastard,' screamed at him, giving no respite. Few could have known his soul-shattering grief during those agonising moments.

Lily! What about her? Had she witnessed his humiliation? Did she really love him? His head beat painfully. His veins were conveying sand and pebbles to his brain, and they hit against his temples, striking at his sanity. God! The pain! At that moment Danny hated every living creature. Maybe all Lily really felt was pity!

Oscar tried to alleviate Danny's misery, but his deliberate impartiality in the matter only made his wisdom sound ornamental. After being disgraced, who wants to hear about fraternal love? Oscar helped none but to drive Danny into a world of repugnance. And this new emotion was strong, and wild!

Somir wasted no time. He wrote the note, feeling a thrill in disparaging Lily. Up to a point anyway, for his real intention was to secure the good graces of Mr Serwall, through whom Lily could be his! He signed his name with curves that would have amazed even Merlin, and instructed Sam on how to present the envelope. Afterwards, they retired to the creek with rum Somir had stolen from his father, and had themselves a ball.

The next morning Oscar answered a rapping at the front door. He found himself face to face with Serwall. The man reeked of liquor.

'Where's Danny?'

'In bed ... what's up?'

'Listen,' Serwall's lips twitched. 'I want that little nigger of yours ...!'

'Hold your horses!' Oscar flared, 'What's going on?'

'That boy of yours isn't going to make an ass out of Lily!'

'Danny?' Oscar was genuinely surprised.

'You heard me! And this isn't the first time. He isn't fit to clean Lily's shoes!'

'You're entitled to your opinion,' Oscar snapped back, 'Only understand this. I'm Danny's guardian. If something's wrong, I'm the man to see. Don't you go around threatening him – get that clear!'

'Well, let me say this; if I ever catch that – that *thing* with my daughter, so help me, I'll wring his blasted neck!'

'Look, Serwall, either you sober up, or I'm going to get pissing mad!'

Serwall stared at his man. 'I'll remember this!'

'I hope you do!'

Serwall turned and left, and heard the door slam shut behind him.

Rosita swallowed. She moved towards her husband and placed a hand on his.

'What's Danny done!'

'I don't know.'

'Oh, Father,' she sighed, leaning on Oscar's shoulder.

The upshot was that Serwall left for Bartica to see Latchman, a businessmen, to procure a husband for Lily. Latchman's eldest son, Dianand – a likely suitor – worked in the civil service, and his father's financial backing provided ample security for Lily. Once an agreement was reached, she was as good as married.

Serwall spent half an hour brooding over Lily's shocking conduct before he finally stormed into her room. What happened on that hill! Nothing, daddy. Did she do anything wrong? No, daddy. Did he touch her? No, daddy. Did she understand what he was asking? Yes, daddy. Didn't she know that the thought of a nigger for a son-in-law would drive him insane? Was she mad? No, daddy. She had dragged him into the filth with this disgrace. Did she know that? Did she know he was going to crucify her? Slut!

Oscar grimaced after tasting Rosita's stew.

'Get lost!' She shoved him gently against the wall.

'But you haven't answered me,' he protested. Rosita was serious when she turned to face him.

'Move to another place perhaps? My dear Oscar, it wasn't my decision to abandon the city. It was *ours*. Before your fortuitous pools win you found fault with the neighbours, you said they were aggressive, you said the noise drove you insane. You said "too much dust on the road from too much traffic". You said exhaust smoke made you sick. You said it was a steaming rat race, and we would be mad not to get out of it when we had such an opportunity.'

He stood smiling down at her severe but humorously accurate criticism.

'I'm only saying this for us,' she continued. 'I love you and I know what you want from life. Mahdia was your dream village, and it was mine when I set eyes on it. Surely this thing can be sorted out between you and Serwall? I think he'll see things straight when he sobers up.' She paused to take the rice off the fire. 'Are you really intending giving up all this, the village, our whole life here, just because we've come up against a little opposition?'

Oscar stiffened. 'You heard what Serwall said. You saw how those – those miserable vultures beat the hell out of Danny. What am I supposed to think?'

'Well, as far as the fight is concerned, boys always will get into scuffles. I had four brothers who were always

41

fighting and they'd end up with the most horrible bruises.' She shuddered. 'I don't like the thought of what's happened, but I think we should dig in. What makes you think it'll be different anywhere else? By the way, have you spoken to Danny?'

'Yes. He didn't say anything.'

Did you speak to him seriously?

'Well, I asked what caused the fight, hoping to lead on to Lily, but he's badly shaken. I don't think he wants to discuss anything at the moment.'

'You must talk to him, you know that?'

He sighed. 'Tomorrow is his birthday, you know that?'

Rosita hesitated, then smiled. 'Yes, I see what you mean.'

'And you may be right. It's probably all a false alarm,' he added hopefully.

'Oh, Oscar, I don't mean to attack you, but I do like it here. It's peaceful and the air is fresh and good. Where are you going?'

'Back in a moment.'

He found his pipe in the bedroom and began to assemble it. Blast! Why did this have to happen? He hated complications. He opened a drawer and took out his tobacco pouch. Yes, Rosita was right, the stress-free conditions of this rural life had shown in her face after only two weeks here, and he himself felt so much healthier. Even Danny loved it.

His thoughts wandered on to Danny, their first meeting and Danny's shy, mild manner. How at first he withdrew when Rosita made to touch him. The adoption procedure. How he himself had felt when Danny first called him 'Daddy'. It was so good to have someone to instruct in that delicate art of fishing, someone to rear in his world of literature. He was interrupted by Rosita.

'Oscar, can you give me a hand with this stupid oven?'

'Coming.'

4

Today was his birthday. Danny awoke with excitement in his veins. He scrambled out of bed – in spite of his aching muscles – and changed gently, threw his pyjamas on the clothes-horse, and was soon through the back door into the grey, chilly morning. Mist enveloped the village, obscuring the trees and houses, concealing the insects that scurried about the red footpath, plunging all colour into one magical hue. The grass everywhere drooped with the dew. He accidentally nudged his elbow on a stave and uttered a sharp cry, blowing on the spot, but it was a stinging reminder of his humiliation. Yet, he was happy.

Somewhere near Pepper Hill a cock crowed hoarsely. From the depths of the forest came the experimental whistlings of waking birds, the amusing gibberish of restive monkeys, and the usual multiplicity of noises of insects. He sighed peacefully. These familiar sounds forever awakened joy in his heart. He walked with measured steps, bathed in the tranquillity of the land, the sweet chill before the dawn, and heard the patter of dew drops on leaves blanketing the forest. Over the bulk of undergrowth, the mist hung like drapes, with that mystical quality of transcendent beauty. No dust, no children running and bawling, no Somir to pester him. Somir! The bully! Danny promised himself that one day he would set the records straight … one day!

He was walking faster now, listening to the creek rushing on its merry journey to the mighty Potaro, swishing along the banks, teasing the reeds, gurgling contentedly.

He was half-way up the road when he noticed it, barely a bonfire in the east … the flame of a new-born twilight. His jaw hung, and his heart swelled like the pink glow over the dark-foliaged horizon, and all his aches were washed away. If only she could see this dream called sunglow! Hushed were the moments his soul merged with the heavenly light, and his love could have filled the ocean.

Like tidal waves Mahdia's roads ran. Leisure walks, consequently, were ill-advised. Frustrating, though Danny sometimes welcomed it, was the unpredictability of the weather. Heavy downpours – even as the sun blazed out of the sky – were common, and the size of the raindrops was marvellous!

From his vantage point he could see their cottage, and the red, flowering flamboyant that stood in the back yard like a giant umbrella. Their house looked so unreal in the distance, a wooden structure in some fairy-tale.

He walked until the road levelled off like a plateau. Here stood a few dilapidated buildings in which marabuntas, spiders, crickets, rats and other crawling things had taken up residence. The breeze blew steadily here, and nipped at your face and neck, and pressed your shirt to your skin with icy fingers.

Danny hugged himself but shudders continued to pace his body. The plateau sloped a hundred feet and beneath, to the north, stretched a deep valley, crawling with vegetation. Westward the great hinterland unfolded, green on green, mountain on mountain. He stared at the picturesque landscape, wishing he could conceal it from unappreciative eyes.

If only Lily were here!

Far beyond the green, rolling expanse of jungle, far beyond the tors and knolls that lay like oversized turtles, the distant haze clouded mountain peaks that would appear monumental, majestic, immediately the sun climbed over the sawari. He would brave the chill rising from the valley to gaze at his mountains for, indeed, he felt convinced he was a part of them, or, perhaps, that they had once been a part of him.

The mysteries of loneliness unravelled here. Commanding the untamed world he adored, his soul became vibrant. But a sigh escaped. One day, please God, let him bring her to experience what his mind's eye beheld. The wind whistled. He dug his hands into his pockets, hunching his shoulders, but already mild rays of sunlight were piercing the leafy crowns overhead.

A door creaked agonizingly. Danny started, and glanced behind, but scolded himself for imagining things. Then he heard a commotion in the sky, looked up to see a great flock of ibises on their northbound voyage, and marvelled at all that scarlet against the silent blue.

Often had he witnessed expressions of awe on the faces of tourists who visited the hill. Bald-pated, bespectacled men whose heads shone like mirrors; tall ladies with craning necks and fluttering eyelashes; squat, barrel-bellied cigar-smokers whose prolific chatter put the village parrot to shame. Not to mention those hairy, undersized legs and knobbly knees in gaudy shorts!

He wondered about these foreigners. What they really felt. They knew everything about pyramids, physiolatry, soil erosion, and horticulture, and always associated this or that scene with one they had encountered elsewhere. Upon hearing their forty-legged adjectives, Danny used to shrink away, distressed that they were tagging his beautiful land, categorising, and thrusting it away in some dust-filled cabinet.

But one day his land had announced her authority. She replied through the wind, the earth, and the heavens, and her epithets were shattering. Rooftops went up like kites, houses rocked, trees were devastated, the sun went dark and – to his immense delight – man, the imposter, the insignificant, was exposed.

The roaches and worms his visitors scorned – weren't they the very creatures that feasted on us after we were lowered into the cold, waiting mud? Whether we were born in the miseries of poverty, or on pinnacles of fame, didn't they devour our bowels with equal fervour? Even the summits displayed the same unconquerable grandeur, long after the climber was gone – a new challenge to a new race.

A piece of glass glinted, reminding him of the time. He turned to face the sun that having sneaked up behind a dukali into a sparsely clouded sky, now swept the village clear and radiant.

At the edge of the cliff he imitated the booming call of

the howler, smiling as his echo ricocheted along the valley. Then he felt it. A really solemn urge to shout out the name of his beloved; to hear his valley repeat it – a sort of testimony to the love he bore.

But why? he asked himself gravely, she knew! He made to leave but something heavy weighed upon his heart, and a voice within sharply rebuked, 'Surely it isn't asking too much!' A bead of perspiration formed on his forehead, and a terrible silence reigned.

'What kind of love is it that is afraid?' questioned the voice, 'Go on, prove this thing you boast!' The vice of guilt tightened, and an elbow of conscience nudged him from behind.

'Go on, shout it!'

Sweating, his confusion dominated by misgiving, he walked shakily back to the edge. He looked down, and a lump formed in his throat, but he folded his fists determinedly, closed his eyes, and laboured, 'You know I love you, Lily!' Barely audible was his affirmation, no echo resulted, yet all the land seemed to sigh with relief.

He jumped when a canary whistled suddenly, and glanced up to see if the bird was not, in fact, Lily's guardian angel spying on him. How he regretted her absence. To see Mahdia in slumber. He felt confident he had enough strength then, to embrace and kiss her properly as he should have yesterday. If only she were here! Then he thought about the mother and father he never knew, and silently telegraphed a message to all would-be mothers and fathers never to abandon their children if they could help it. He traipsed home, humming his favourite tune:

> '... for my momma,
> and pappa,
> 'cause I want them to know,
> I love them so.'

Oscar sat barefooted on the back steps, whistling as Danny approached. Danny had guessed that a surprise lay in store for him – he wasn't sure what – but all those whisperings and endeavours at silence whenever he appeared, had to amount to something!

'Been to see your mountains again?'

'Yes, dad.'

'Oh ... happy birthday!'

Needles of joy pricked at Danny's breast.

'Thanks,' he said, and squeezing past, one hand on Oscar's broad shoulder, he felt the urge to brush Oscar's curly hair.

'Your breakfast is on the table, and when you're finished, I have something for you.'

Wide-eyed with enthusiasm, Danny started for the table.

'Hey, wait a bit!' cried Oscar. 'You've got to wash first, eat *all* your food, then you'll qualify for your gift.'

Danny looked so crestfallen, he added, 'I'm sorry, but we musn't make Rosita unhappy, she's put a lot into preparations.'

With a pseudo-serious expression, Danny ate, swallowing his eggs and sandwiches with incredible urgency, but slowed down to savour a slice of mango. Then he gulped the coffee.

Rosita worried about Oscar's gift. She had been praying, whatever it was, Danny would show no dissatisfaction. She wished she could share Oscar's confidence.

Danny had often heard people remark that Oscar was a disciplinarian. That he was of the old school, stubborn. 'Principle', he would insist, 'it's a matter of principle'. With Oscar it was always a matter of principle. Yet, compared with the other parents in the village, Oscar was tops! Then he remembered the short pork-knocker – his rescuer. Yes, Lloyd was tops, too!

Danny used to emulate Oscar, but one obstacle forever frustrated him; his hair could never form that silky, wavy pattern typical of Oscar's hairstyle. The thing wouldn't budge! Nevertheless, he had some consolation. In the breeze Oscar's hair blew madly, and when it did, causing him to fret and blow air through his nostrils, Danny would look up at him, and pat his own 'wool' affectionately.

At last he finished. He rushed into the kitchen, plunged his hands into a basin of water, and dried, wiping his mouth in his shirt sleeve. Oscar stood waiting, gift in hand. He pretended to be examining Danny for signs of careless washing, and smiled when he noticed a crumb on his nose.

Both he and Rosita were dumbfounded at the pains Danny took to unwrap the birthday paper. As he peeled off the last piece of tape, Rosita glanced anxiously at her husband.

'Oh, gosh! The *World Book of Animals*!' Danny flew up from his squatting position, hugging the thick, oversized volume, kissing it, then rushed over and threw himself into their arms. 'You remembered! Oh, boy, he remembered! The book I showed you in Booker stores. Mom, he remembered!'

Danny was back on the floor, the tome opened, and he was turning each page so carefully one would have thought the words might tumble out. He exclaimed at every colourful illustration with little 'oohs' and 'wows'.

Rosita was moved. So, Oscar was right. Her eyelashes were wet. Oscar moved over, placed a hand around her hips, and led her away. In spite of the prevailing happiness, Oscar knew he had to approach Danny, to steer him clear of further clashes. He knew Danny's sensitivity would make his task all the more difficult. A major decision was required and his primary concern was Danny's education.

Danny was so occupied with his book, he neglected to feed his chicken. It wasn't until he heard the bird pecking away furiously at the wire mesh that he realised how late it was.

At six, he padlocked the coop, and went upstairs. Blancmange, chow-mein, custard, and patties were in the making, and everywhere there was sweetmeat to pinch. The tangy smell of essence lit up the scene.

'Hello,' Rosita greeted, 'see, all this for you tonight.'

'Great!'

'There's a letter for you.'

'Really?'

'Yes.'

Out of curiosity Rosita had opened the unsealed envelope. That curse so often associated with women had overpowered her. Was the card from Lily? It bore no signature, except for the word LOVE. She was drying a plate when Danny entered the kitchen frowning.

'I wonder who sent this?'

Rosita asked the old disinterested, 'You don't recognise the handwriting?'

'No.'

A smile played on her lips, 'I wonder if ... No, I don't think Oscar would... .'

'Dad?'

'Hmm.' She glanced at the card again. 'Sure you don't recognise the writing?'

'Honest.'

Oscar laughed at the idea but insisted it wasn't he. The matter was soon forgotten, for supper was served, and what a fattening meal that proved! Danny struggled from the chair, Oscar belched with undisguised satisfaction, and Rosita spoiled herself.

A thin line of smoke was rising from behind Oscar's newspaper when Danny paused to look at him before retiring. Some day, he promised himself, he'd have a pipe of his own.

He closed his own door, put down the mosquito net, and climbed into bed. Before tucking in, however, he noticed the statue near the blue, enamel washbasin. He slipped out, and sat on the floor, for his knees still ached. With reverence he prayed, like the nuns in white habits who cared for the orphans. He asked Jesus to bless his foster parents and, 'If possible, Lord, make them my real mother and father. God, only You know how I yearn for real parents. And, Lord, could You make them a trifle brown-skinned?'

Then he remembered Lily. Lily! He jumped to his feet, and was soon tumbling out objects in his cupboard. Out came his prized book. He flicked through the pages and found the card. Now he cradled it in his arms, and the viciously beautiful thing called love swooped down, and sank its claws into him.

Sometimes, Oscar would recite poems of the world's greatest loves, or explain that *the* love story, penned by an 'immortal' was, in the eyes of its society, a downright disgrace. The restless society that burned martyrs for their faith or screamed infamy at an *affaire de coeur* while – not surreptitiously, of course – Lord He-Haw took Lord Haw-He's wife to the ball, and other places. The same society in whose closets dangled the most colourful skeletons. They who decried bloodshed as barbaric, only to replace it with the more sophisticated, and 'civilised' germ warfare. Everyone has, at sometime or other, felt the sting of society's scorn, Oscar often consoled. Yes, his foster father knew a lot!

These thoughts flashed through his mind as he gazed at the sacred card, and deep within, the velvety wings of love flapped against his heart. That Oscar's poems, or talks, meant anything to Danny would be wrong to assume. His love story was uncomplicated. 'Lily,' he soliloquised, 'my own Lily!'

That night he tossed under the blanket. Dreams kept repeating themselves. He dreamt of the large, wooden orphanage and saw, as pellucid as life itself, that hawk-nosed nun who advocated rigid rules and regulations – the she-wolf of the institution. Every orphan hid from her in terror. In his dream she advanced, her cane raised to strike, her lips cruelly set, and he woke with a start, his breathing laboured, his body wet, his eyes staring. Even awake he felt her presence, and could picture that funereal building.

He wiped his forehead, and lay back gently on the damp pillow, grateful that the 'battleaxe' had only been a mental apparition. There were happy times in the orphanage, yes, but the nuns were convinced that the only path to salvation led through Confession Street, for to die suddenly, say, without absolution, meant certain damnation. This often disturbed Danny for, if true, few would ever see those pearly gates.

Then the love magnet drew his thoughts to Lily. Many

of the older orphans had told him of the visit of a princess to the West Indies. They swore she was a living doll. One boy, for want of words, said 'Man, she wasn't real!'

But for him, Lily was the only flower that ever bloomed. Her hair, long and thick, was an object of profound admiration among the women. It fell to her hips in waves, and those with short hair sighed wishfully, and promised themselves to grow theirs just as long. Many did accomplish this feat, but the men gave them no rest, for no shampoo, no quantity of curlers, or brushing, could stem such remarks as, 'Lady, what happen to yoh head?' or 'Woman, watch out foh dem hungry horses!' That did it! Long hair was promptly declared out-of-vogue.

Not far from his window a flock of blackbirds cawed at the rumblings in the starless night, and from the jungle a toucan honked sadly. Beyond Pepper Hill, Horatio lifted his broad head and howled – an endless ghost-luring sound – and Danny disappeared under the blanket. Before the cuckoo clock struck ten, he was fast asleep.

5

Danny soon realised that something wasn't right. Both
Oscar and Rosita were unusually quiet. Neither had said
much since breakfast. Twice, he caught them speaking in
undertones, and even noticed Rosita observing him slyly.
Was he imagining things? He had never seen her purse
her lips like this, and Oscar's abstract, almost cold stare
unnerved him.

As the day progressed, things worsened. Danny passed
Oscar in the living room, conscious that the newspaper
shuffled to permit those blue eyes a view of him. Was it he,
then? Had he mashed someone's foot? Their eyes were
trained on him like the muzzles of loaded guns. Once he
attempted to speak, but that seal on Oscar's lips! Did one
pat an enraged baboon? Or call 'puss, puss,' to a
wounded lion?

That night, he slipped into a troubled sleep, constantly
waking at the slightest noise. Finally, too restless to sleep,
he counted the nails in the ceiling, contemplated the holes
in the mosquito net, and lauded the intricate patterns of
the rafter grains. Was Mary his only Mother? He gazed
absently at the compassionate smile, then sat up and
stared, for the smile seemed to widen mockingly before
his eyes. For one fleeting moment Danny thought he was
going out of his mind.

The next morning he sighted Lily leaving the parlour.
Somir was loitering near the bridge. Danny craned
through the window. Somir winked at Lily but she cut
him a glance that could have halved Goliath! He sighed.
At least he could depend on her. Then he noticed Serwall.
The teacher stood grimly on the other side of the road.
What was going on?

After supper, he found out. Rosita lit a lamp, went into
the kitchen, and Oscar appeared from the hall. He stood
before Danny, like a life sentence.

'I'd like to have a word with you,' he said, and

beckoned to the sitting room.

It was so sudden, somewhere in Danny's stomach a muscle twitched, and when Oscar pulled up a chair noisily, his bowels sprang water. He didn't really sit when asked to, it were as if his legs had collapsed.

'Tuesday was your birthday, and Rosita and I didn't want to upset you – especially after your fight with ...' Fight! Danny caught the word; you call that a fight? '... and I think it's important we discuss it. I was hoping that things would blow over and that Serwall would apologise for something that happened between us recently. Unfortunately he hasn't.'

Then Oscar released the bomb. 'It's about Lily.'

Danny's stomach flew to his throat. His mind raced. He bowed his head and stared at the floorboard. Oscar was saying, 'Mr Serwall looked mad when he complained.' So that's it! He might have known Somir wouldn't sit idle.

'Want to tell me about it son?' Oscar probed gently.

Danny's eyes were fixed on the floorboards, and the more he stared the more beautiful the wood appeared. Now there was nothing! His eyes had gone blank. But wait! this was rude, not speaking, not answering Oscar. Yet, what could he say? Silence was inept, yes, but he lacked the *sang-froid* to explain things as they really were. Oscar walked up to his packed-to-capacity bookshelf labelled 'classics' – his reservoir of knowledge – and cleared his throat. Danny looked up, their eyes met, and, for what seemed the first time in centuries, Oscar smiled. He stiffened, applied a match to the bowl, and pulled on the pipe. Smoke filled the room.

'The famous personalities in these novels,' he began, his index finger indicating a row of books, 'have had their share of hardships.' The finger stopped. 'This man was a great author – a reformer – a man whose works to this day remain an inspiration to aspiring writers, painters, and poets; one whose characters have walked play-houses the world over. He left a literary heritage, yet died a pauper.

'This one – on the other side of the globe – was an inventor, among other things. He risked his life to prove his theories. Today his genius manifests itself in many present-day luxuries, and some of his inventions are essential to our so-called 'modern civilisation', but who gives him a thought when they erect a lightning-rod to protect their home?' He broke off for a few puffs and smoke bombarded the ceiling like Indian signals.

'This man was an Archbishop; to many, a martyr. He died for what he believed in. And here we have a celebrated painter who fled his home town because of a woman. The point, Danny, is that each man has his problems. The road isn't always rewarding, it isn't always smooth. What is your story? I'm sure the blame isn't all yours. Why not tell me about it? I promise you, I'll give you every moral support.'

In the kitchen Rosita raised an eyebrow in admiration. That certainly wasn't what Oscar had been rehearsing. She wanted to applaud and giggled inwardly at the thought of Oscar's expression after he was made to look ridiculous.

Oscar wished Danny would speak. Serwall's threat stood foremost in his mind. This matter had to be ironed out, and fast! Danny couldn't afford to miss school, not with his remarkable aptitude for learning. But Danny held his ground with the obstinacy of a cow on a busy country road. The altar-lamp burned steadily, and under the table Paddy, their Siamese cat, carefully bathed his paws. The continuing silence defeated Oscar and he later agreed with Rosita that the subject was probably too emotional for Danny.

Danny sat looking at the radio after Oscar left. A new battery stood beside it, ready to burst into action, but the receiver was dead. It had been for days. They occupied the stand like old friends. He couldn't imagine why these objects should arrest his attention. When music was drifting through the house, he never even paid heed to the attractive, green, indicator light. Why should the radio communicate with him now? Immediately the wet leaf of fear licked at his neck. Had he become psychic? Or was he going mad?

He stood up, his heart pounding, and reached for the set as if it were an explosive device. Trembling fingers touched the bakelite knob. He turned the switch. Click! Then nothing! He felt like kicking himself. Even Paddy scampered off when he tried to stroke him.

In his room he knelt, opened the tiny swing doors of his cupboard, and picked up Lily's postcard. One thing was certain, he'd never betray her … Never! Besides, didn't she promise to marry him when they were old enough? With this hope he sought to console himself, but a miserable loneliness beyond the scope of thought, loneliness vaulted in fear and confusion, that he might lose her, lose everything, caused him to sink to his knees in agony.

Imagine Somir's chagrin when he discovered that his letter – instead of standing him in good stead – helped only to sink his plans with all the subtlety of a torpedo. With Danny he stood a chance of winning Lily; now his hopes were dashed! Serwall meant to marry her off with frantic expedition. He had not anticipated this ugly twist of events. He stood on the threshold of perplexity, seized by fits of anger and frustration. His cunning scheme was back-firing in his face with all the stench of sulphur.

Nevertheless, this harrowing experience helped to sharpen his senses, and made him even more determined to realise his dreams. If he could gain Lily's confidence, he reasoned, Serwall might rescind, at least, delay the wedding, for surely these precautions were because of Danny. Why should Serwall have any objections to him? Wasn't he, Somir, an East Indian, and a Hindu?

Rosita picked up a pan of dough and pushed it into the box oven.

'You sure Serwall's planning to marry her off?'

Oscar was reading a newspaper on the step. 'Yep,' he answered.

Just then a little girl ran up.

'Good afternoon, Mr Thorne, Mr Savory ask if you could go over for a minute.'

'Okay, Dolly, tell him I'll be right over.' The girl smiled, tiptoed, peeped into the kitchen, and dashed off. Rosita laughed. She had grown accusomted to the natural inquisitiveness of country folk. Oscar got up, scraped the bowl of his pipe, and left it on the sideboard for Rosita to clean.

'I'll only be a short while.'

'But I'll soon be finished with the baking.' She pretended annoyance.

'So? We aren't going to eat just yet.'

'I know, but I thought you said you were going to lovey-dovey me?'

Mock incredulity masked his face. He moved over, grabbed her by the shoulders, and kissed her roughly.

'I never said anything, fibber, but for that, I'll make certain I'm back in five minutes.'

She stuck out her tongue at him, and he wagged a finger.

'I'll settle you!'

'You'd better!'

Smiling mischievously, she watched him go, knowing that in spite of what he preached, he found her desirable in these moods, and such wisdom was an ace in every wife's hand. She dreaded the thought of his finding out that Rudolph had again been provoking her. Had been throwing out challenges, insinuating that he, Rudolph, could teach her a thing or two if he caught her in bed.

She felt contempt for the 'young upstart' as she referred to him, and knew, with Oscar's temper some things were better left unsaid. Rumour had it that Rudolph was with every 'passable' female in the village, and she wondered whether indeed Mrs Welsh could look with favour upon such a vile egocentric. Nothing would have given Rosita greater pleasure than Rudolph's public disgrace, perhaps to strip him naked, and place him in stocks, or tar and feather him, as in some old customs.

Oscar found Ben bathed in smiles.

'What the hell're you grinning at?'

'Wanna guess?' Ben handed over a letter. 'Go on, read it.'

It was from José, the diamond agent. In six short sentences the man expressed his disposition to continue the business with Ben, regardless of the consequences!

'Ben! You lucky brute!' Oscar expostulated, squeezing Ben's hand. Ben guffawed, and leaned back contentedly.

'If the profit's the same, I promise I'll build that chapel. It's something Charles always wanted to do.'

'Yep, I remember. Believe me, the village needs it badly.'

'Men like Sugars might be converted,' Ben ventured.

'Him? Never! He would convert the angels!' Oscar retorted.

'Who knows?'

'The unhappiness he's caused!' said Oscar, reflecting how uncomfortable he felt whenever Rosita mentioned Rudolph.

'The pork-knockers say he's like a horse!'

'I don't wish to discuss that!' Oscar said bitterly.

Suddenly Ben cried, 'Look, Rosita's calling,' and Oscar glanced up.

'All right, I'll go give her the good news,' then, remembering, he inquired, 'Does Fielder know?'

'Yes, he was here a few minutes ago. He was pleased.'

'I'll bet he was. We must drink to this.'

'Any time, man, any time.'

As he headed home, Oscar couldn't help reflecting on Rudolph, nicknamed 'Sugars' by the very miners who watched him like a hawk. Rudolph's exploits and escapades lived on the tongue of every villager. Slim, good-looking, and with his wavy hair, his Clark Gable moustache, many a woman saw in him the full-blooded man of their dreams.

He never worked, yet he wanted for nothing. Some suggested he was a mulatto; others claimed he was a gaucho, that his father was a Spaniard, and his mother an Indian. He himself couldn't be bothered by genealogy. Once women blushed in his presence, or swooned in the fragrance of cologne that forever lingered in the wake of his footsteps, that was it. Even those who professed to loathe Sugars secretly yearned to discover his 'way' with women.

Because of their pride, however, these men approached

him only when intoxicated. The result? They ended up buying drinks they could ill afford, and became so loquacious, all that was required of the philanderer were encouraging nods, and the poor miners invariably forgot their mission, until the following morning when their error dawned upon them with a reality more sickening than their hangover.

Naturally, their contempt for the level-headed Sugars grew and – coupled with an understandable fear for their marital security – helped to shorten tempers. Oscar wished the man would leave Mahdia. Imagine! he had even offered Rosita a chocolate bar – the nerve!

Rosita opened the door, her frolicsome mood gone.

'Better have a word with Danny.'

'What's wrong?'

'I don't know. He's crying in his room.'

The door was locked. Oscar rapped. 'Danny ... Danny!' There was no reply. 'I'd like to talk to you. Please, open the door!'

After a minute there was a shuffling of feet, then a click. The door opened. Danny stood, choked with tears. No sooner was Oscar in the room than he fell upon him and embraced him.

'Take it easy! There, sit and tell me about it.'

Danny continued to sob loudly. Rosita stood outside looking on in distress, but Oscar slyly motioned her to leave. Then he spotted the letter. He picked it up and read:

'My dearest Danny,

'I don't know if you heard what happened to me. Dad found out about us, and beat me until he was exhausted. He said he hates all negroes. But I don't care! I'll always love you no matter what! He's arranging for me to marry Dianand, a schoolteacher in Bartica. Please remember, though, I'll always be yours in my heart. If you were old enough to take me away, I'd go willingly, and suffer anything to be with you.

'I am in possession of a book entitled The Holy Bible, and I read about your Jesus in a section called the New Testament. He's really a wonderful person, Danny. I'm positive I could make Him my God, if you desired. I have welts on my back which I pray will heal; I'd hate you to see them.

'No matter what, I love you, I love you.

Lily

P.S. I hate Somir!'

Oscar folded the letter, and stuck it in Danny's shirt pocket, placing his arm around him.

'I don't know what to say. In matters like these, time alone can provide the answers. From all appearances, Lily will soon be married ... I'm sorry, I thought you knew.'

Danny shook his head, wiping his eyes.

'Don't worry! You'll see, things will work out. You're a brilliant lad, with a terrific future! Look, there'll be other Lilies in the world.' Oscar spoke with determination, but the head nestled under his arm shook with a futility few would recognise.

Rosita looked at Oscar. 'You think it's wise?'

'I've given it a lot of thought. Look, Serwall is Danny's teacher – there's no telling what he'd do to spite him! Besides Danny's too clever to waste more years in his crummy school.'

'When do you plan on taking him to town?'

'Tomorrow. I'll explain the position to the dean; Danny's reports will speak for themselves. They can even give him a test if they like.'

'What if – if it doesn't work out?'

'If the dean hasn't been replaced, there's nothing to fear.'

'Friends in high places, eh?'

'Why not, we all need them at some time.'

Rosita turned to leave but Oscar grabbed her apron string, and pulled her back. She tottered backwards into his arms, laughing.

'Don't go falling for Sugars while I'm away, or else!'

'Flattery will never blind me to the harsh realities of life ... you should know that!'

He squeezed her around the waist. 'Flattery may not

succeed, but chocolates are quite real.'

'You think I can be bought?' She pouted her lips. He leaned forward and kissed them.

'Politicians claim every man has his price.'

'Yes, darling, but not every woman.'

With tears blurring his vision Danny packed his grip. A teardrop fell on the floor near an ant, and the insect halted, erected its feelers searchingly, then scurried away in panic. Yes, he shook his head sorrowfully, fear had found its way into the heart of even this insignificant thing that, perhaps, in a swarm of millions, was a mighty warrior. Outside, darkness was rapidly setting in. He knew that when the dawn broke, it would be the last sunrise he would witness in Mahdia for a very long time.

He thought about Serwall, Somir, and Sam! God – he loathed them! Inside his bowels coiled like snakes in agony. When his eyes beheld the statue, he asked. 'Mother of God, can you hear? *Why me?* Is it because of this?' He pulled at his hair. He was still crying when he got under the warm bedcovers. Between sleep and wakefulness, he saw Lily's face appearing and fading, her lips moving, but he couldn't hear the words. All through the night he groaned, dreamt of Serwall's huge, misshapen mole, and the grinning masks of Sam and Somir. In the morning when Rosita shook him, he felt as though his neck couldn't support his battered head.

The preparations, the anxiety, the chattering, the promises, the farewell, none of these helped to mitigate his sorrows. Peter, Mahdia's number one driver, and Oscar made a joke of everything they saw, without success. For Danny, never was a journey so empty!

The constant jerking of the lorry which, upon a time, he relished, was a curse, for his breakfast churned and swelled in his stomach like chunks of cardboard. 'Pray,' Rosita had urged, 'And God will answer you. Be strong.' Well, he did ask God to stop the wedding. Yet – as the distance between them grew with each passing mile, as the tears puffed his eyelids – he knew that his strength was founded on Lily's love.

How did one calculate love, label it, and stack it away for any number of years? What mathematical formula was employed, and with what did one equate it so that its depth, middle, could be known? How did one remain tranquil when every fibre in one's body screamed to touch the face of one's beloved? How did one endure the agony of despair? Even if the world were to rise in his defence, Danny knew it would not fill the void in his heart.

Lily, tears lining her cheeks, soaking her lashes, blotting the pages of the grammar book before her, strove mightily to obey her father, to concentrate, but her greatest effort mocked her. How could she love someone else? What was the point of this arranged marriage?

Her hand reached for *The Broken Wings* and slowly she turned the pages. She believed, if reincarnation existed, Kahlil Gibran had known her nearly four decades ago! Shakespeare had written about her one hundred and fifty-odd years ago!

The sound of footsteps startled her. She glanced behind to see her father, a glass of wine in his hand, his eyes glassy.

'Soon, my girl,' he half sang, 'you'll be a bride. Every girl's dream! Dianand is a fine boy – decent, East Indian, like your father, your mother, your grandmother, your grandfather. One day you'll thank me. Wait and see, all you believe now will be different when you grow up. You'll see how miserable Blacks are. You think they could ever change? Never! They want pity, attention, fine clothes, plenty of money, and you give them! You give till you can't give no more.' He paused to swallow a mouthful, then his eyes narrowed, 'And what? They reel back on you like wolves for what you haven't got. There's no exception; women, this,' he held up the glass, 'and music ... that's a nigger in a nutshell!'

No! she wanted to protest. Danny isn't like that! But she couldn't. Hers was a weakness laced with the narcotics of futility. She sat insensibly, listening, not hearing.

When she visited the parlour that afternoon, Lily was

unaware of the observing eyes. And that evening when she took the clothes off the line, the same eyes watched intently. She tied up the hammock, filled a bucket at the vat, then retired for the night.

Somir grinned in the shadow of a coconut palm. Once his approach was correct, she was his! He couldn't rush things, yet he couldn't relax, for Lily's engagement would materialise in a matter of weeks! With Danny absent, their union was as inevitable as tomorrow's sunrise.

6

Plans for the wedding were under way, but the phantom of disaster was already looming. One sultry, full moon night, Somir fell victim to restlessness. He pushed his hands into his pockets – his first long pants – and paced the yard like a mouse fresh in captivity. That Danny Thorne was out of the picture was a tremendous relief. Furthermore, Serwall would prohibit any communication between Lily and Danny. Out of sight, out of mind, thought Somir, pleased with himself.

But – and that splinter was causing a lot of pain – Lily seemed unaware of his existence. Twice he had offered good mornings but on both occasions she ignored him completely. Why? He wasn't ugly! In fact, he rather fancied himself good-looking. Besides, he had a light complexion, better than Danny's. What the hell was she playing at?

Perhaps Sam's suggestion, that she was playing hard-to-get, hit the nail. After all, what pride could she have left? She had already desecrated herself by being in the arms of a nigger! Didn't she know there were girls more beautiful, more cultured, than she? Once she had scorched him with her eyes, but even then she had only succeeded in sending waves of elation up his spine. Her eyes were … well, he didn't deny she was pretty!

Somir's imagination soared. Think! The whole of Mahdia regarding him with profound admiration. Somir, the man who swept Lily off her feet, snatched her from the jaws of matrimony, saved her from disaster, then made her his blushing bride! His name – pouring out of the mouths of the aged, falling upon the ears of generations – would become a legend.

He was contemplating this image when the murmur of voices reached his ears. It came from behind an arbour near the secret footpath, and sounded quite close. The silvery tongue of Sugars was wagging. Then Somir detected another voice – a woman's! Silently he crept along the shadows until he reached a fallen tree, and peered into the dark.

In the moonlight he easily distinguished two forms. He strained his eyes against the night but could not identify the woman. Suddenly she turned, just as a cloud parted allowing the light to fall on the attractive face of the wife of Mahdia's most popular diamond-seeker. She was giving Sugars a stringed leather pouch. Somir couldn't believe his eyes. She? Was it really she? The proud Mrs Welsh, sneaking in the dark with that notorious lover-boy Sugars?

'These diamonds ain't worth much, lovie,' Sugars said, fingering the stones, then delicately weighing the pouch. Excitement gnawing at his inners Somir sneaked along the grass like the very ocelot the village feared. Soon he was as close as he dared.

'It's the best I can do!' he heard her reply.

'Listen, your man made a big haul. I heard 'bout it.'

As he spoke he moved up and took her somewhat roughly in his arms. Somir's eyes and ears strained.

'Let go!' she cried, 'I hate you!'

'Why did you come, then?'

'Because I was afraid of – of what you might do. I tell you, Morris is bound to find out I've been pinching his diamonds. He'll kill me!'

She tried to free herself, but Sugars held her firmly, one hand steadying her broad hips. Then, softly, he began to pour his formula of woman-weakening epithets into her ears, his high-scented lotion adding that aphrodisiac touch so vital for his *coup de grace*. She struggled to wrench free.

'Keep those words for your whores!'

'You are my whore!'

He easily controlled her efforts to break free, her beefy body pressuring the seams of her skirt, that part of her anatomy about her loins rolling with each shift.

'Rudy, don't! You wouldn't dare … not here! Please!'

But his hand was already up her skirt. He pressed her to the leaf-strewn ground in masterful command.

Pangs of fear gripped Somir. He had never witnessed

anything like this, but his eagerness for such intelligence made him resolute. He continued to watch, bursting with excitement that one so youthful could handle such a full-blown woman; within the half-hour during which Somir's breathlessness nearly suffocated him, Rudolph unknowingly demonstrated what several books on the technique of sex could not have accomplished.

Morna's underwear lay in a surprisingly small white heap only metres from Somir's grasp, and Rudolph's winning of it had been a work of art. Somir's blood ran hot. He had learned an invaluable lesson. In matters of the heart the strong-arm method yielded the finest results. Didn't Mrs Welsh call Rudolph a bastard? and a beast? But afterwards, didn't she cling to him with eager lips, and arms, and legs?

His face irradiated by the scheme in his heart, he checked the calendar, and circled a date. When the thin moon reigned, he would strike.

October 13th was Fatima's pilgrimage. Rosita, Oscar, Fieldor, Sergeant Hopkinson – the new lawman who had replaced old Corporal Cummings – Serwall, Lily, and many others took part. It was a solemn occasion. The bigger men carried the marble statue of Our Lady of Fatima on stout, wooden staves while the procession followed, sweetly singing the hymn that commemorated the event.

People of all religions participated, and those Amerindians without a 'religion' fell into line, some giggling, others simply overcome by the gravity of the occasion. In their natural habitat Amerindians are a silent, watchful people.

The procession was half-way up Pepper Hill when, not far away, Sugars cornered yet another gullible housewife, and soon had her sprawled like a plaything. But all the while his thoughts dwelled on Rosita. She'd snubbed him repeatedly, but one day he'd get between those meaty white legs, and when he did, he'd fix her good!

The screaming continued. People were scampering in

every direction. Clouds of dust leapt into the air as if a giant beater was thrashing the road. Two forms were locked in mortal combat, their spitting, snarling, snapping, tearing and biting slowly drawing a fearful, wondering crowd. They were seized by trepidation, and fear that the ocelot might leave Rex and charge at them instead. Sam stood wringing his hands, panic contorting his face. Rex had his canines deep in the ocelot's neck, while the latter had secured its claws in the Alsatian's shoulder. Then Rex tripped, and over they went, off the road, down the slope, on to the grass, grappling fiercely, their battle cries hair-raising indeed! Ugly wounds dripped on both, but the cat's neck oozed scarlet. Rex's nose was split to the bone. They parted, circled each other ominously, growling and caterwauling, the ocelot's paw spread like a cobra's head. Rex's fangs, gums and spittle were a truly daunting sight. Again they flew at each other's throats, and again, each time colliding like wrestlers on all fours.

Oscar tore off towards the bungalow without his shirt, shouting the alarm to Ben who obviously hadn't heard the din. Up the steps he bounded. 'The gun! Where's the gun?'

'Wha-what the devil!' Ben had to wheel hurriedly out of Oscar's way.

'The gun!' Oscar's eyes interpreted the confusion outside.

'There, behind the door – cartridges in the drawer. What ...?' demanded Ben. Nervous hands grabbed the cartridges.

'Ocelot!' spluttered Oscar, and was gone.

Fieldor, seeing him running past the parlour, leaped over a drinks box and was soon hurrying towards the crowd. Oscar raced on down the road, the gun pointing at the heavens.

'Give way, give way!' he announced his arrival, and on seeing the shotgun, Oscar's seemingly uncontrollable anxiety, the people scattered like stray dogs under a shower of bricks.

Perhaps it was because he had Rex, and the gun, on his

side, but Oscar's courage was something to laud. He rushed into the fray, and thrust the muzzle between the madly tumbling forms, with not a thought for his own safety. This intrepid feat did the trick. The ocelot wrung itself free, and dashed for cover, but it was not swift enough!

The blast caught it in the rump, pitching it into the air, landing it between the bushes, and the blood that spilled over the green leaves began to drip here and there. Something of an apocalyptic torpor followed, and it was some time before the people huddled around, but no one seemed anxious to venture into the bushes to confirm the ocelot's death. They spoke in hushed tones, and pointed, and said that the cat was as dead as anything, but kept their distance.

Rex advanced. His legs wobbled, and folded under him, but he struggled up gallantly, looked at Sam and wagged his tail weakly. The crowd followed, and found the ocelot looking so still and harmless, some laughed that 'such a lil thing could frighten anybody!'

Jim was a poor taxidermist, but he managed a good enough job, and the people presented the skin to Oscar, who later admitted he wasn't sure he had been holding the gun right.

Everyone subscribed towards the vet's bill. The man feared for Rex's life, but the dog pulled through, though he was never the same again. In appreciation the people sent Sam gifts of money and viands. One man presented him with two cute ducklings. Then a gold-digger suggested a fiesta and everyone agreed, and everyone downed tools the next day. They killed two sheep, and rum flowed, and there was much singing and dancing. Sugars seized the opportunity and Morna Welsh again fell victim, offering no resistance as the youth handled her in bed like a schoolgirl.

Four days later two children discovered Sugars' body near the cemetery, one shoe off, bloodstains over his shirt, a wooden phallus stuck in his mouth. Sergeant Hopkinson promptly transferred the cadaver to Bartica, where it was buried. Relieved, the lawman wrote, 'Case closed, insufficient evidence,' in his personal notebook, and made out his report with a 'praise the Lord!' indication.

Sugars' notebook turned up later. The sergeant tried to keep it a secret, but he was shocked by the ribald's memoirs. Names and the sums of money he had extracted from them headed the pages, and there was Rosita's name – his 'last obstacle'. Of the other women Rudolph had kept a progressive record of his successes, carefully observing the women's 'fancies'; Rosita's weakness was described as 'having an adventurous disposition'.

The sergeant burned the book, and Rudolph's autobiographical sketches darkened the day. But secrets being what they are, it would have profited Hopkinson to publicly announce the contents of the book, for soon a verbatim account of it was galloping through the village.

The thin moon arrived on October 23rd, and true to his word, Somir set about his task. Lily was dipping her second pail when he strode up and confronted her.

'I – I want to talk to you; don't make no fuss, please.' She stepped back.

'Somir? What are you doing here?'

'Just – just to talk. I know your father is in Bartica. I got something to tell you. ....'

'Well, I certainly don't wish to hear it,' she said, swinging away with the bucket. This knifed into Somir. He sprang after her, but his only intention was to make her listen.

'Please,' he pleaded, grabbing her wrist, 'you must listen!'

'Let go,' she cried, dropping both buckets – one almost on his foot – and tugging free. She darted upstairs, Somir in pursuit, and he was just in time to prevent her shutting the door. In a moment of hysteria, Lily erred. She slapped him violently, and it stung, and not only his face! The bitch! She slapped him, but kissed a nigger! He caught her hair and pushed her to the floor, stifling her cries with one hand while he tore vengefully at her clothes with the other. Lily resisted stoutly, clawing his face, kicking, and he hit her. She bit his hand, and he hit her again and again. Even unconscious, Lily was irresistible.

Sergeant Hopkinson shook his head.

'Never rains but it pours!'

Sister Baldeo, a self-appointed clairvoyant who made excellent black-pudding, nursed Lily. Oscar and Fieldor kept vigil in the kitchen.

'Did she say who did it?' they asked when Sister Baldeo appeared.

'Somir,' came the reply, and the sergeant started to pace the floor agitatedly, knowing that this outburst of crime wouldn't go well for him. Fieldor wore a 'woe unto someone!' look. Hopkinson left the house and returned an hour later.

'Somir's gone,' he said. 'Not a trace anywhere.'

'Where can he go?' asked Fieldor.

'Any guess is a good one,' returned Hopkinson, scratching his head with his cap hand, 'but boy or no boy … this is rape!'

Oscar looked at Fieldor blankly. 'Nothing we can do this minute.' He made for the door, followed by the others. Outside, Rosita was ascending the steps.

'How's she?'

'She's okay, missus,' Hopkinson held the door for her, 'but your presence will be welcomed.'

'I'll see you later,' she said, smiling at Oscar as she passed.

'Serwall's going to kill Somir,' Oscar predicted.

'Not if I can help it,' promised Hopkinson.

There was still no sign of Somir the following day. All the men in the village got together and with an Amerindian guide, entered the forest, returning hours later without Somir, but with a diversity of insect bites. 'No tracks,' insisted the guide, and they retired for the evening, weary, sticky, and suspicious of the guide.

Oscar complained that his feet were sore.

'Wish some coffee?' Rosita greeted him with a smile.

He slumped into a chair, 'Thanks.'

'Oh, I forgot', she said, 'Serwall's back'.

When Oscar remained silent she continued, 'Would you believe it? He hasn't spoken a single word. I'm frightened, the way he stares.'

'What do you mean?'

'Well, he just sits and ... stares! Even Sister Baldeo's left the house.'

Oscar sighed, then turned and stretched. 'I'm tired, and I need a bath. Tomorrow I'll have a chat with Serwall, or rather, see if he'll talk to me. You finish the coffee?'

'I've only just put on the water! Did you hear Rudolph had me listed as a possible "prospect"? It's a shame somebody had to kill him.'

'Are you starting that again?'

'Well, he wasn't a bad-looking lad.' Rosita took a step forward.

'You feeling okay?'

'My! don't tell me my hero is jealous over a dead man. Look, darling, you men have such complexes about other men.'

She went briefly into the kitchen.

'Here you are, sir, your coffee.'

He hesitated, shifting indecidely. Then she winked down at him, and fluttered her eyelashes provocatively, and he accepted the saucer with a boyish sulk.

'Who'd believe that the man who slew a monster ocelot', she pointed to the cured skin, 'could get worked up over a dead playboy!' She placed her hands akimbo, but tilted her hip suggestively.

'Don't push your luck!'

Slowly, the months passed. Serwall, a shadow of himself, spoke to no one. His afternoon walks – and he rarely returned before twilight – took him away from the village, and he was frequently seen talking to himself. No one bothered with salutations. He walked with his head low, his eyes vacant. The wedding was postponed, then cancelled in a 'sweet' manner, but Serwall knew no Hindu family of any social standing would accept Lily after her disgrace.

His ego ripped to ribbons, the shell of that proud,

cunning Serwall came and went like a zombie. Every evening they watched him, a man of melancholy mien, and every day he looked a month older. Everyone agreed there was something unhealthy about Serwall's silence. Consequently the school fell to neglect, and many parents appealed to Lily to pick up the pieces.

Ben invited Oscar to see the short list of materials remaining for the church.

'How's that?' he asked proudly.

'Tremendous!' encouraged Oscar.

'Work'll start soon as the timber arrives.' Ben clasped his hands. 'It's the least I can do for the Man up there. He gave me the strength to fight back.'

Oscar nodded.

'I see Lily's a regular at your place.' A knowing smile crossed Ben's lips.

'Yes, she and Rosita chat about Danny all the time!'

'Strange how God works,' said Ben, adding 'does *Mr* Serwall object to her visits?'

'Naw, he doesn't object to anything!' Then Oscar caught on and smiled wryly. 'Yes, strange, isn't it?'

Ben sighed. 'I hope it works out for them. Seem's Danny's really proving himself. This should teach old folks not to meddle in the affairs of young people. Why hasn't Danny visited yet?'

'He says if he met Lily it might upset his study programme. He's writing four O levels next year. Judging from his mid-term results, it wouldn't surprise me if he got all four. My friend, the dean, is impressed with him.'

'Does Danny know about Lily?'

Oscar sighed. 'No, I'm afraid not.'

When Somir realised what he had done, he fled from the village. He crossed the creek, scrambled up a ravine, and was soon stumbling into the forest. Night closed in fast, and the quarter moon shone to no avail. He ran on blindly, bumping into saplings, tearing his flesh on thorns, tripping over lianas, falling into sap, getting up and stumbling again.

Exhausted, sweat and mud falling from his body, he sank to the ground. Insects chirped deafeningly, owls hooted madly, and the air was clammy. Darkness greeted him on every side, so black, he couldn't see his outstretched hand. His brain pounded insanely. Everything smelt of blood ... of Lily!

Somewhere a twig snapped, and Somir knew fear as he had never experienced before. He screamed as the ensuing silence leapt upon him like a gigantic bat. He hugged himself, choking on his sobs, his head fixed between his knees. Then the ink of the forest swallowed him up in its impenetrable bosom, and his hairs stood on end as the ice of fear penetrated to his soul.

7

Oscar and Rosita had their first quarrel. He wanted to go hunting with Fieldor and Sam, but she opposed it bitterly.

'What's happening to you of late? You're always running off somewhere. If it isn't draughts, it's fishing, or hunting, or … or maybe Morna Welsh! You must be the only man she hasn't captivated yet. Or has she?'

'Don't *you* judge anyone!'

'Oh, I see! I've become questionable!'

'How would I know? No one tells me anything. But since we're on the subject, yes, someone did say they saw you talking to Sugars at our back door. You never told me anything about that! Damn you, Rosita. Can't I trust you – even you?'

'Sugars? Me? Oh, I see!' she said, suddenly remembering. 'When did you hear this?'

'Some weeks ago. Before he came to … before he was found dead.' His voice fell but his breathing was laboured, and his blue eyes were half concealed by low, dark brows.

'Is that why you've been neglecting me, treating me like this?'

'What do you think?'

'Why didn't you ask me about it?'

He turned his back on her angrily.

'If you had told me like a proper wife, I wouldn't have to ask!'

She walked up to him boldly. 'All right. I take the blame for this, and yes, I – I had forgotten to mention it after Sugars's death. I had considered the matter closed.' He moved away but she turned him to face her. 'It hurts to think you could suspect me.'

'How would you have felt in my place?'

'You don't know, but I've tried to hide a lot from you in the past. What you found out was only by accident. I knew you had a vile temper, and I knew what could have happened. I was frightened for your safety. Since that time with the chocolate, I realised how dangerous you could be. I didn't want you to get involved with that – that man-whore!'

Oscar folded his arms in a gesture of defiance, but he was all ears.

'Once when you were in Bartica, Sugars came and rapped at the back door. I was cooking. He greeted me decently. I thought he came with a message.' She went silent.

'Well, what the hell did he want?'

'Look, Oscar, don't get worked up over nothing!'

'What did he want?'

Rosita looked terribly embarrassed. 'He – he said … I … he … believe me, Oscar, it was all – all filth!'

Oscar was swelling with anger. 'Are you going to tell me or not?'

'Stop shouting at me!'

'Are you sure he didn't come into this house …?'

Rosita's hand flew upwards before Oscar could finish, and the slap left him like a man petrified. He gazed after her in astonishment, slowly, his hand on his face, the spot warm from the impact, he followed her into the bedroom. It was the first time he had felt her fury.

It took him a full hour of coaxing to get her talking again. Apparently Sugars had come to inform her of a cure for barren women.

'What cure?'

Rosita flushed. 'Why are you so insistent? It was just a lot of sex junk!'

'I'm sorry,' he said gently.

She looked at him, the hurt in her eyes only too evident. 'Now go back to whoever "saw" Sugars with me and find out if they didn't see me slam the door in his blasted face! Well!' Oscar cleared his throat. 'Let's forget it! I'll cancel my hunting trip.'

Each fortnight without fail Danny's letters arrived. His last one contained his first G.C.E. certificate. As they had hoped Danny excelled in all four examinations, clinching distinctions in two science subjects. The dean had said that the exam was merely to determine the students' weaknesses. An experiment.

A further letter from the college stated that Danny was unquestionably scholarship material, and would Oscar give them permission to start preparing him for the arduous task ahead?

He consulted with Rosita who swore she hadn't a clue, but said that if he, Oscar, thought it would be biting off too much, she would go along with his decision. However, she added, if others could do it, why couldn't Danny?

Oscar didn't want Danny to end up a 'screw-ball', so he replied that if Danny did well the next year – if he passed all eight subjects – he wouldn't hesitate to give his sanction. Ordinary level was one thing; writing three subjects at advanced level was no joke. Not when candidates had to train their sights on distinctions. No, Danny must clear the hurdles one at a time.

In the village few could keep abreast with the changes that were taking place. Sam had become a diligent worker, and was able to relieve his father altogether of the cattle business. Many had thought that when it came to finance, Sam would crack up, or run off with the money, but his stability in every transaction he made, the way he worked himself mercilessly, his complete control at the helm, left everyone flabbergasted.

Fieldor remarked that the metamorphosis began when Somir disappeared. Sam had blossomed into a fine young man, and rumour had it that 'a lil' chick in Bartica was responsible foh he transmogrification.'

Ben Savory on the other hand, became fanatically religious. Construction of the church had been delayed because of inadequate conveyance for the uprights, floor beams, and rafters, but when finally they arrived, Ben went wild!

Every day thereafter he could be found sitting in his wheel-chair, in the broiling sun, sweating, shouting, signalling, and nodding with the professional air of an architect, while four carpenters hammered and sawed away with demoniacal dedication. Even as the village cynics shook their heads, Ben's church started to make impressions against the sky. In the evenings Bible sessions were held on his lawn, and an almost phosphorescent sign said: DO NOT PICK FLOWERS.

Quite a few Amerindians became devout Christians, and it wasn't long before the villagers requested a minister. They applied in March, and in June a jolly, plump, bespectacled clergyman showed up. He was received with reverence by an over-enthusiastic Ben who gave him temporary living quarters in the bungalow.

To everyone's amusement Ben fed the minister, an expatriate, like a king. By the end of the second month the man had gained a stone, and developed a frightful paunch. Naturally, the children imitated his ungainly walk at every opportunity. One day, in a small gathering, the minister glanced down at his stomach, and remarked, 'Goodness gracious! I'm beginning to look like the milkman!' And everybody laughed. Comforts being such delightful monsters, the rectory was never completed.

Oscar was chopping firewood when he heard Lily's scream. He planted the hatchet, and raced over to the house. Serwall's body dangled from a rope when he burst into the house. Oscar's quick thinking saved the day, and Serwall was soon stretched out on a bed, mumbling incoherently.

'Thank God he's alive!' Oscar praised.

Lily busied herself with warm rags, wiping his face and neck, while Oscar massaged his shoulders and legs. The entire village converged in minutes, and everyone knew that the poor man had failed in his suicide bid.

Oscar knew Serwall had been acting oddly, but never dreamed he would go to this extent! Lily clasped her father's hand in hers and cried. Oscar put the place back in order.

It was some time before Serwall's lips moved, and large tears coursed down his temples. 'I don't want to live!' was what he was saying, 'I'm finished!'

'Look, man!' Oscar charged, 'You're not finished, and believe me – there's plenty to live for!'

Lily started to sob when Serwall took Oscar's hand and kissed it, pleading, 'Ask Danny to forgive me.'

After Serwall's breakdown, Lily re-opened the school, and with the assistance of an ex-headmaster, was able to further her studies.

The village welcomed the change, for Lily had a way with children.

Sergeant Hopkinson had long abandoned his search for Sugars' murderer. He knew that whatever the villagers knew, he'd never find out, for it was the custom of village folk to shut up like a clam if some secret or other needed dire protection. From the answers he received Sergeant Hopkinson concluded that every man in the village knew who killed Sugars. To him this was tantamount to saying it was either all of them, or none at all. Whatever the case, the men looked rather pleased with themselves.

As for Somir, he remembered him only when he had to look up his 'Missing Persons' file.

One day, however, a group of children were down by the creek enjoying themselves when a ragged, bearded man approached, cupped his hands, and drank like a fugitive. He glared at the children, splashed his face with water, then withdrew furtively into the bushes.

Naturally, the children elaborated on the description of this 'bogey' man. And lied, so that even grown-ups avoided the area. The man's glare became the fire-shooting breath of a mythological beast; his matted hair they equated with Medusa's. The darlings built up an image so horrifying, they themselves were afraid to venture near the spot. But the mysterious figure continued to frequent the creek, appearing stealthily in the afternoon shadows, retreating with the sunset, and the children never ceased jumping up bawling out in their sleep.

Rosita answered their new doorbell.

'Oh, hello Lily! Come in. How's daddy?'

'Better, thanks.'

'I got a letter from Danny today. Did you receive one?'

They went into the bedroom.

'Yes.'

'He's going to tackle eight O levels next year.'

'I know.'

Rosita sat down with a darning needle and began to mend Oscar's fishing denim. 'Think Danny'll get through?'

'I know he will.'

'How's it with you two?'

Lily kept her gaze downwards. 'Fine ... I think.'

'What's wrong?'

'Well, sometimes it seems so long. As if he'll never come back.'

'Oh Lily! That's so absurd! Do you realise it's already three years since Danny's been away? Think, another two years or so and it's all over. Look, love, the way things are going, one has to have tons of paper to get a decent job. If it weren't for our good fortune, I don't know where we'd be! Harder days are ahead, Lily. Every day Oscar complains about rising unemployment, or about the stiff competition facing school leavers. Danny must want for nothing, neither Danny nor you, for that's the way we think it'll be.'

For a moment it seemed Lily would spring up and dance across the hall.

'Anyway, what I'm saying is, be patient. You two love each other and time's no enemy at your age.'

'What if he meets someone ...?'

'We women are so suspicious! You must know Danny! He's not the type. I'll wager my neck on that. By the way, you never told me you used to meet Danny by the creek after dark.'

Lily laughed. 'Did he say that?'

'Yes. He wrote enquiring about the place – whether things had changed much – and he mentioned something about "unforgettable moments" he spent there with you. Ah-ha! Come now, Lily, out with it!'

Lily did not answer, but her eyes had a happy, faraway look. After a while, as if their secret escapades had reminded her of something she said, 'Do you think I should tell Danny about – about ...?'

Rosita smiled awkwardly. 'Well, it would test his love, but I shouldn't tell him just now.' Lily nodded in silent agreement.

Later, in the kitchen, Lily began to rinse the dishes against protests.

'Do you think he – he'll hold it against me?' She asked suddenly.

Rosita suppressed a momentary fear. 'Goodness, no! People in love overlook such things … besides, it wasn't *your* fault!'

She had barely said these words when Lily rushed over and hugged her. 'There, there,' she comforted, stroking Lily's hair, 'You're much too beautiful to be worrying about foolish things like that. Everything will work out, it always does.' Lily squeezed Rosita all the more. 'Oh, Mrs Thorne, I'm so ashamed of myself. And now – now that dad tried to – to …'

'Your father wasn't well, love, but he'll be okay, just wait and see. This is what life is all about; you mustn't lose faith.'

Danny and his friends left the college and walked briskly down High Street.

'Where to?' asked a freckled-face, red-haired lad.

'Brown Betty, most noble McTurk,' said a boy they called Chubby.

'Anyone for banana-split?'

'Sundae is me,' said Danny.

On the pavement McTurk ran a geometry ruler along the iron rails of the old Victorian Law Courts, making it sound like the staccato fire of a machine-gun.

'Hey, Danny, when you gonna teach me judo?'

'When you grow up.'

'Hey, George,' the lad stopped hitting the rails, 'you think Felix here can tackle Danny?'

'Listen, you instigators!' cried Felix, 'you know damn well Danny's the college champ!'

'Wasn't what you told that girl at the party,' reminded McTurk, his freckles all the darker for his grin.

'Oh, shut up! Just 'cause you couldn't get a dance.'

'Hurry up,' implored Chubby, 'I'm starving!'

'What you plan on having, Chubby?' asked Felix, whose cap had lost its ensign.

Chubby's eyes rolled. 'Think I'll have a hamburger, milk-shake, and a patty.'

'What? That's all?'

'What'd you mean, "that's all"? You think I'll stuff myself so's I can't enjoy the chow-mein, fruit juices, and custard afterwards?'

'Push him over a cliff,' advised Roger.

'Hey, Danny, when you gonna take us to Mahdia?'

'Soon. I – I promised myself not to go back till I've finished exams.'

'That's all right, but we're dying to see this dream village.'

'Me, too,' confessed Roger.

Chubby's teeth sparkled. 'I want to see a particular person there. Bet she ain't half the fairy he's making her out to be,' he jerked his thumb at Danny.

'You'll see! you'll see!' promised Danny.

Inside the restaurant they pooled resources, and Danny queued up at the cashier's cage. Roger made for the jukebox.

'How much?' Danny asked an attractive cashier.

'Seven-fifty, handsome.'

Danny paid, blushing, and went to the counter. He stood waiting to be served when he heard the tune that forever softened his heart. Immediately his thoughts strayed into the beyond; he was looking but not seeing. His soul hummed to the music:

> '... 'cause I want them to know,
> I love them so ...'

'Can I have your voucher, please!' repeated an aproned girl, irked.

'Sorry, miss.'

The girl went off mumbling something about 'the young men of today owny livin in ah dream world!'

Danny turned to observe Roger who was leaning on the jukebox like a cowboy. One day he'd bring Lily to listen to this very music machine, to the very selection being played:

> 'I'll walk a mile, with a smile,
> For my momma, and pappa, ...'

Across the eating hall Chubby, holding his stomach, pleaded, 'Where's the morsel?'

'Please hurry up, you guys,' someone shouted, 'this human caterpillar's dying.'

Finally the day everyone had anxiously awaited arrived, that of the annually celebrated donkey race, and after the generator installation ceremony, where many a long-winded toast put some junior members to sleep, this sporting event was a welcome diversion.

Fieldor made his contribution to the village in entertainment for the unemployed. He purchased a movie-projector, a skittle set, and a ping-pong table. Ben Savory donated two expensive dart boards, and four sets of arrows. Oscar supplied indoor games, including chess, scrabble, and ludo, but only the ludo and snakes-and-ladder games were ever employed, and some claimed that the Amerindians stole the wooden chess pieces to use them as ornaments.

Because of the heartening response, Fieldor extended the parlour to accommodate a small dance-hall, much to the elation of some pork-knockers who seemed to treasure Saturday-night brawls. Other diggers wrote profound poetry, and when they got bored, went off to Bartica in search of a prostitute.

For months the organisers of the race had promised a day of enjoyment – indeed, they had been extremely active. A roar of excitement greeted the Bartica competitors. Betting and rum were the order of the day.

One pork-knocker, Charles, showed his confidence in Bartica's pride, Mathilda, by placing two hundred dollars to ten in that donkey's favour. Let it be said for the powerful Mathilda, she was justifiably called a 'noble ass'.

Her victory was something of a foregone conclusion.

Nevertheless, Mahdia's die-hards backed Kid, the village filly. Kid was notorious for his playfulness, however, so his supporters betted cautiously, for Kid – while the contest was in full swing – would not hesitate to desert to go bounding after Horatio.

An elderly villager stroked his grey beard and watched with some degree of amusement as three men tried to push a frightened donkey down a plank bridging the road and the back of the truck. The animal's ears stood stiff as cardboard. Two blackish, marble-round eyes protruded in terror and there ensued an undignified braying for mercy. Deafeningly the ass brayed its forelegs rigid, the veins on its ears swollen, its whiskered nostrils drawn back revealing nightmarish incisors. Naturally, the more they pushed, the more the animal resisted.

Mathilda followed and immediately one could detect an animal of class! Surefooted, she graced the gangway without assistance and stood aloof like the queen of asses, not deigning to rub shoulders with the others.

The riders quickly assembled. Spectators formed parallel lines along the road, in sun-hats, visors, or with handkerchiefs tied round their heads; the women used parasols. Children munched on sweetmeats. Horatio was present, but kept his distance, as someone was bound to stone him sooner or later.

The noonday sun bathed the village in warmth, but stimulating was the fresh forest-scented wind combing the luxuriant undergrowth near the valley's edge, cooling the faces decked with perspiration, ruffling shirts and dresses. Rosita and Morna stood out for beauty and figure, and many wives caught their men admiring these two in their close-fitting jeans.

Up the road, a pother caused by Rex chasing madly chuckling hens sent several cows trotting off in alarm. Minutes later a tar-black pork-knocker (his friends called him 'Polish'), strode up, his shirt and khaki pants sweat-drenched, and held up his hand.

'Ladies and gentlemen,' he roared, 'de long overdue jack-ass race is 'bout foh start. De favourite, Mathilda, a virgin donkey, will today stamp she authority as de fastest female in de land.'

He stretched and rolled his eyes comically, and his nostrils expanded with amazing elasticity. The spectators laughed so heartily their sides ached, or they coughed, and choked out their laugh. Somebody sneezed, and a few glanced back to enquire of this extraordinary musical instrument.

Exclamations of approval rose grudgingly from the Mahdia crowd when Mathilda strutted out from under the shade. Then came Kid. He pranced and back-kicked a few times before settling down, and set the crowd roaring again. Someone shouted, 'Is who rub black-pepper in he backside again?'

Unlike Mathilda, Kid was neither glamorous nor well covered; but he wasn't bony. Sam, who contained Rex on a leash, cried, 'Bus she ass, Kid, show she you is a real road-runner!'

All the time Horatio watched, and waited. Kid was the only living creature who acknowledged that he, Horatio, was not a 'demon' dog. Often the one could be seen tearing after the other over and around the village, while farmers wept at the sight of their kitchen gardens and fences. Today Horatio looked determined to duplicate such an extravagant excursion only, of course, Kid was so engrossed with those noisy humans!

A hush fell as a young lad mounted Mathilda. For Mahdia, John Ramjohn would ride. John weighed about fifty pounds and for Kid, this was not excessive.

The boys looked nervously at the starter, waiting for the flag to descend, and when everyone was quite breathless with excitement – down came the flag, accompanied by hundreds of cheering voices. The race was on!

Rider and animal were required to cross a white line near the cemetery, turn, and head back towards the crowd. The first one in would gain the coveted silver trophy. Both started shakily, but Mathilda took to the front, her muscular hind legs working vigorously, her jockey urging her forward.

Kid quickly took his cue from Mathilda, and went

bouncing down the road. As they neared the bridge, up went the cries of 'Atta girl, Mathilda!' or 'Come on, Kid, dig up!'

The pounding of hooves was the only sound which meant anything to Horatio. His tail started to wag furiously, and unbounded happiness shone in what were previously two dull, neglected eyes. 'Here I come!' he seemed to shout as he sped down the hill, straight for the donkeys.

Mathilda might have been swift; she might have been reliable – but dogs! Mathilda and fowls, yes! Goats – maybe, but dogs! Visions of horror flashed before her! Worse still, Horatio, with his blood-shot eye, his broad nose and red, overlapping gums wasn't everyone's version of a fun-seeking animal.

Mathilda saw this black thing charging at her and, like a train braking at eighty, she down her forelegs. Pebbles went up like sparks, the rider catapulted through the air, and Mathilda, slipping and sliding in terror, took off in another direction!

Bartica's supporters charged after her, with lassoes, bamboo sticks, or, like Charles – with hundreds at stake – cursing. But they merely succeeded in chasing the terrified beast into a farmer's garden.

Tears of laughter turned to tears of sorrow for some, as Mathilda sent clumps of vegetable and fruit trees flying high, and left several churned up flower beds in the wake of her flight. Ben's beef-red cheeks retained their elevation until the animals, snorting and yelping, headed for his flower garden! He gaped at the catastrophic horde, but Mathilda missed his beds, as did her enthusiastic disciples, and Ben mopped his brow in relief.

Kid had never failed to amuse, but Mathilda was something else! Round and round the bungalow they went, two other dogs joining in the extravaganza; down and down went the kitchen gardens, higher and higher rose the tumult until hoarse, many subsided to wipe their tears.

Charles lost heavily, for Kid alone completed the distance, and the visitors walked around looking enraged. Charles swore he'd kill Horatio.

Not until the sun had set was order restored. Fires were built near scout tents, and those totally inebriated snored disgracefully in the open. Some sang 'Etaname' and 'Sitira gal' or blew harmonicas until they, too, collapsed and advanced the snoring orchestra.

Towards the close of day, Rosita was casually leaving Fieldor's parlour when she overheard two drunks discussing Sugars. How he had possessed terrible dimensions, how even the prostitutes dodged him. Rosita had almost forgotten him. Conceited devil, did he really think she was not woman enough? The fool. She wondered how he would have felt if he had known Oscar was quite a man!

Later that evening, Oscar detected an enraged voice, went over to the bedroom window and peeped through the jalousie. There, at the far end of the village, he espied Charles, stick in hand, storming up the hill, shouting, 'So help me, I'll kill you, you bitch!' Across the way, where trees, and twists in the road hid the cemetery, he heard the sorrowful ululations of the village stray.

'What's up?' Rosita rolled over in bed.

Oscar shook his head. 'The old story, never put all your eggs in one basket.'

'Shouldn't there be a nice ending to a happy day?' she asked.

'Of course. Why?'

'Well, I still have this powerful desire to be manhandled on a table.'

'Since you returned from the shop you've had nothing else on your mind!'

She smiled. 'Women have their whims, darling.'

'You're telling me! Sometimes I wonder whether whims are assets or liabilities. Are you sure you haven't got a touch of "nymphoitis"?'

'Whatever is that? Anyway, you read five nights a week, what's your excuse?'

'All right, but can't it wait till tomorrow?'

' "It" has this terrible twitching that's hard to ignore,' she said, pulling her negligée tantalisingly up her smooth, shapely calves.

'Why a table?'

'The better to serve it, darling.' She was naked under the garment.

He got up. 'All right! I'll never understand you!'

'Don't try to, just love me!'

Immediately, her manner changed. She was crying. He knelt down beside her.

'What's wrong?'

'I feel so – so neglected. So unwanted. Oh, Oscar, just hold me like you used to.'

An oversized toad swam across the icy creek, crawled out sluggishly and with two ungainly hops settled on the white sand, its gargoyle head a fitting trophy for Mathilda's efforts. A branch fell nearby and from within the undergrowth two red, incandescent eyes stared.

At that moment, anyone looking out of their window might have seen Somir raiding a fruit tree in Ben's garden. Might have caught him prowling around the bungalow, or sneaking into Fieldor's coop, gently pocketing eggs while two hens clucked disapprovingly. Might have seen him tiptoe painfully across the thorny ground and grab a shirt from a nearby clothes line.

But no-one raised the alarm and Somir disappeared like a whiff of smoke.

That month peritonitis carried away the milkman. Tiny died in great pain, and those who had had so much fun with him during their childhood, and the tots who had added new dimensions to the song 'Ting-a-ling-a-ling,' placed wreaths on his coffin, and shed tears of remorse.

The minister read the 'Dust to dust' bit with profound solemnity, but ever so often was caught glancing down at his stomach in alarm.

8

Ben proposed that they use his place and he and Oscar invited Serwall, Mr Brown – the minister everyone addressed as 'reverend' – the sergeant, and a few others for a get-together.

'Indeed,' the minister swirled his whisky, jingling the ice cubes in his glass, 'it's rather an achievement – eight O's with four distinctions! Don't you think so, Mr Serwall?'

'Ooh, yes. In my time we had the matriculation examination and that gave some of us hell. Yes, eight O levels at one sitting is a commendable effort.'

'I drink to that,' Fieldor said quietly, and glasses were raised.

'To Danny!'

Oscar made a toast to the success of the diamond business and Rosita tapped her heel on the floor.

'Hear, hear!' Up went the glasses, though Serwall had looked a bit uncomfortable during the speech.

'Tell me, Mrs Thorne, will Danny be calling it a day? Perhaps planning to take up a trade?'

'Oh, no, reverend; at present he's writing three A's'.

'My, that is something!'

'How's the new transmitter working, Fieldor?' asked Oscar.

'Great! I'm beginning to wonder how we ever did without it.'

It was then Ben made an announcement. The church was going to be opened to the public that coming Sunday. That it would be officially announced tomorrow. Everyone started to clap. Mr Brown looked terribly pleased.

'Have you got your sermons lined up, reverend?' someone asked.

'Oh, yes, quite a few!'

One prospector asked if God would listen to a man

who'd never set foot in a church.

'God listens to everyone, Mr Lloyd,' to which Lloyd replied. 'You all ain gon believe dis, but dis is de first time anybady ever call me Mister!' and he looked genuinely surprised.

A few were still chuckling when Rosita raised her voice to be heard. 'Since everyone has something to celebrate, can I drink to my new kero refrigerator?'

'Cheers to dat!' boomed another prospector, then to Oscar, 'Buddy, I hope yoh like cold plates,' and there was much laughter.

'I see there's a newcomer to the village,' said Serwall.

'Yes. He's an American, I believe,' said Ben.

'That's right,' added the minister, 'He's Mr Jack – something. Sister Baldeo was telling me about him. I think you'll be seeing a lot of him, Ben.'

'Why's that?'

'I heard he wants to try his hand at prospecting. It appears he was told that the roads here were paved with gold.'

'Well, everybady got dem own luck,' someone reflected, 'Sometime de man make a big strike first time, while we old hands still brocking we back foh pay foh we ration.'

'True, true; let we drink to dat!' cried Lloyd.

'Jack took some supplies from me,' Fieldor put in, 'but from what I gather, he's only out for the thrills.'

One man whispered something to Oscar who looked at him in consternation, shook his head and opened his eyes in gestures that charged, 'You don't say things like that in front of a minister!'

Naturally Rosita had to find out what had transpired, but Oscar – knowing her unpredictable nature – deigned to tell her only when they were safely out of earshot.

'Imagine,' he stressed every syllable, 'He wanted to toast to Lloyd who had his "goady cut out" last month! Rosita! Rosita, will you stop laughing! It's not funny, you know!'

'I can't help it. It was the expression on his face; after you shook your head, his smile vanished, and he looked as if he'd just been fired from a favourite job, ha ha!'

Four prospectors emptied bottles of beer into an old khaki-covered cork hat and balanced it in the grass for Horatio to drink.

Hairless patches like charred ruins on his back, a festering sore weighing down one ear, Horatio approached his broad mastiff head low, servile. With his good eye watching their every movement, perhaps for that surprise kick, his tongue skimmed the froth, then he lapped tentatively.

An hour later, his head between the knees of one of his benefactors, his tail gently smacking friendly trousers, Horatio made little noises like a lovesick puppy. A kind hand even reached down and patted the flea-ridden head he offered to everyone. After that it seemed Horatio would go to the end of the world to demonstrate his gratitude.

That night he barked like a thing inspired, sung an oratorio or two, rolled over and over in the middle of the road, and appeared to want to protect the entire village from it – something, anything, everything. Finally, too drunk to support himself properly he crawled under the bridge of Fieldor's shop, curled up like a mole, and snored fitfully, oblivious to the rain that pounded the zinc sheets; and the trickle of water on his head could easily have been the dreamy stroking of cold, angelic fingers.

Somir filled a canvas bag with tins of sardine, half a loaf, a bottle of I-cee, a tattered, coverless book, scores of cigarette butts, and a decaying breadfruit, and stole through the village. The blanket over his shoulder was a prize! It would provide warmth for the cold nights ahead.

In the forest he emptied his booty and ate ravenously. The transistor he had pinched from the minister's window sill played softly at his feet. He built a fire and picked up the book he had found in the lorry. Pictures of wheels, screws, washers, gaskets and pulley-belts greeted his eyes. Dammit! There were no sleeping princesses. No tiny green men! No witches! Dammit!

His thoughts were cut short, for in the nearby thicket something was moving. There were some thrashing sounds, then silence. Something was coming towards him. A twig snapped. There was a screeching noise in his brain! They were searching for him again! In this damn darkness they were searching for him! The fire or the transistor had given him away. He groped blindly for the radio, and his finger accidentally set it blaring. There! It was off! He breathed quietly again, listening. In a frantic moment he considered extinguishing the fire. No, it was too late. He felt for his knife. His heart was thudding in his skeletal frame as he got down flat on his belly. He ignored the soft, wet thing worming its way against his foot. He was trembling. The earth was damp. Mosquitoes were buzzing madly and some were clambering up his nose. He crushed one in his ear. He strained to hear, but the sounds had stopped. He knew why! They had him surrounded! At last – they were going to get him! He was trapped. God, he was trapped! They were going to hang him!

The fever descended rapidly and shook Somir to the bone. The blanket! He had to have it! It lay near the fire. What was that! Something moved suddenly in the grass. Then a scratching noise! The beating of wings nearby. Then silence. He lay listening, his breathing swift, and heavy.

Suddenly a squawking noise pierced the night. Somir's heart nearly collapsed. He looked up and saw movements in a tree, the silhouette of a bird. F-ing parrot! He ground his teeth. God, even the birds were trying to kill him!

Shivering, he grabbed the blanket and dragged it slowly, noiselessly towards him. Then, quickly, he rolled himself into it. His ankle squashed a soft creature that had gotten into the folds. It was sticky, and twitching.

The fever was closing his eyes. He had to stay awake. The noises had stopped. Good parrot! You chased away the hangmen! Just then his friend descended from a high tree and stood near the fire watching him. Hello, Mr Monkey! How are you? I'm fine. I'm glad you could come tonight, there are people prowling about. They're after me again, you know. Yes. If you peep behind that bush you'll see them. Go on! See? No? Sure? Oh, they must have left. I'll get bananas for us tomorrow if you watch. Yes. Yes, please; it's the fever again. It's killing me. Every night at this time. Wait? What are you doing? No! Leave that radio! Oh, all right! Listen to your Indian Melody Time. Stop making faces. He-he! Oh, Mr Monkey, you are funny. You're dancing like a clown! Ha-ha! He-he, he-he! Not like that! Here, I'll show you. Look, like this, see? Look at me, Monkey! He-he!

The bush-turkey looked curiously at the twitching, breathing blanket, at the dying fire, and quickly gobbled up the bread crumbs scattered near the canvas bag. It pecked at the breadfruit, at a cork, then wandered off.

Rosita and Lily chatted while Oscar served tea. She was proud of the tea buns, the most recent of her successes with the electric oven. She smiled as Oscar appeared with the tray. It was ages since he had turned up his nose exaggeratedly at her creations.

He handed out the teacups then lit his pipe.

'Are you practising, Lily?'

'Practising?'

'Yeah, you know,' and he bent down quickly and kissed Rosita on the cheek, like this! For when Danny arrives.' Rosita pushed him off fondly. 'Oscar, stop teasing her. Ooh, she's all blushes now!'

'Seriously, Lily, if you're rusty, and I can help ...?' and pretended he was going to hug her. Lily shielded her head, protesting, 'Mr Thorne, stop it!'

'But you won't know how unless you try,' and he winked across at Rosita.

'Leave her alone!'

'But Rosita, she hasn't done any cuddling since Danny was in short pants.'

There was still colour in Lily's cheeks when Oscar turned his attention to Rosita, squeezing her playfully.

'Will you sit down like a gentleman?'

'No. I have Danny's interest at heart. Look, Lily, this isn't like long ago, when a peck on the cheek would make Danny go all wobbly at the knees. He's going to expect some real action, and you've only got a short time!'

Lily appealed to Rosita who signalled her to ignore him. But Rosita was soon giggling uncontrollably for Oscar had found a feather and was now tickling her ears with it.

'Come on, Rosita, admit it – she does need to practise!'

'Yes, yes!' she shrieked until he let up.

'There. You see, Lily, Rosita agrees. If you're not prepared you could find yourself in troubled waters,' and with that he went off for a fresh supply of tea. Rosita leaned forward.

'Have you written to Danny?'

'Yes, two days ago.'

She thought for a while. 'Love will win out, Lily, I'm sure it will.'

Oscar returned with the teapot. 'Well, Lily, have you considered brushing up on your kissing?'

To their joint surprise, she sat up erect and smiled confidently.

'Don't worry. Danny hasn't been practising either.'

When the stench hit the village no one dreamed of looking under the bridge. When they did, however, it was providential Horatio couldn't hear the indignation and derision they hurled at his bloated, fly-burdened carcass.

The children held their noses and poked at him with long sticks, or threw stones to set the multitude of flies airborne. Fieldor disinfected the bridge and surroundings generously after they removed Horatio.

But he felt the loss, particularly in the mornings when Horatio used to be waiting for him to open the shop, his tail wagging, something of a smile on his face. And he used to follow him about, as Fieldor picked up the besom and swept away the overnight leaves. Later Fieldor poeticised the incident by declaring that, well, Horatio died keeping the bridge.

Danny and Roger left the Metropole cinema and headed for the nearest Chinese restaurant. Roger lit a cigarette, then offered the packet to Danny who, as usual, refused. Both of them had grown into tall, sturdy young men.

Roger, slightly the shorter of the two, aimed the smoke under the restaurant table where he insisted, dwelt an irascible mosquito. They had completed their final examination, and Roger made no pretence about his impatience to leave college.

'I hope this is my final year,' he sighed.

'Did you find the film boring?'

'To tell the truth,' Roger replied, 'the only thing on my mind is the exam. The crap I made of that second paper.'

'Physics?'

'Yeah.'

'Was that why you went to the toilet three times?'

'Look who's talking! You would have eaten your bloody toenails if you'd had the chance!'

Danny couldn't resist a laugh. 'Okay, we're even. Do you realise if I fail, I'll have to remain in town for a further six months?'

'Fail? For God's sake, Danny, at the mock exams, Bradshaw said you were A1 and he isn't exactly liberal with his praise. Added to which, you've been studying non-stop for the past year!'

'So, what about you, you son-of-a-gun! You've never fallen below seventy. Why are you worried? Besides, you never seem to study, period!'

'Ah-ha! But "seem" is the operative word. A technique I employ to save face in the event of failure. Anyway, let the beer flow! What's done is done!'

They drank and laughed, their anxieties fading. Danny even smoked a cigarette.

'Tell me honestly, which do you look forward to more – the results next week or going home to that curvaceous, appetising damsel?'

'That's no secret. After six years, wouldn't you be anxious?'

'True, but there is one secret,' Roger teased, 'and we promised not to keep secrets, remember?' Danny looked away, embarrassment exposing his shy nature. 'Come on, Dan,' Roger persisted, 'you know I like those blow-by-blow descriptions.'

'I told you, we never did it.'

'Never?' Roger stretched the word.

'She wasn't that type. Look Roger, will you get lost!'

They downed two more beers, admired the Chinese waitresses, and winked at them.

'Did you hear that explosion last night?'

'Yeah, I nearly jumped out of my skin.'

'Wonder when we'll be able to sleep on both ears?'

'Will you drop those archaeological proverbs and give me straight talk?'

'Talking pays no toll,' Roger continued, laughing.

'Hope when I open fire with local proverbs you don't fume.'

'Aye!' cried Roger, with his long John Silver accent, 'Two knaves we be, arr, well met!'

One week later, back at college, the art master tapped Danny's shoulder.

'Mr Bradshaw'll see you in his office.'

In his excitement Danny bumped into several boys along the corridor. He knew the results were out. As he darted up the stairs and that familiar door with its frosted glass came into view, a moment of fear gripped him. Had he failed? Would Bradshaw's face have that quiet, disappointed look that made students want to cry if they missed an easy goal on the football field. With bated breath, Danny tapped lightly on the glass, then turned the large brass knob.

9

By the time the broadcasts were heard, questioned, doubted, and confirmed, the people went wild! Danny Thorne had won a Booker scholarship!

'You've got to believe,' Fieldor said flatly, 'the rum's finished!' All he had left was hot beer and in the tropics that isn't to be recommended. He had sold fourteen bottles of XM in less than an hour. That a tiny village like Mahdia could produce a Guiana scholar was too much. Even children's lips were wet by frolicsome parents. Rosita, trying to look dignified, reeled, steadied herself, and sat down in Oscar's lap with a glass of champagne. Then she whispered in his ear, and he rebuked her with a drawl and an unbalanced smile. Serwall reclined opposite them, a glass in hand, one index finger raised. 'It's the foundation that matters,' he insisted.

'All right!' Rosita laughed, 'we give you credit for Danny's foundation.'

Outside in the dark a pork-knocker ranted: 'Read revelation. Revelation is de whole thing, and who yoh tink write it? A John like meself. Yoh tink is fun? Whenevah black man rule he mattee black man, de end near. Watch out for yohself! Don't take me words, though, read Revelation!'

'Gawd!' A gold-digger gulped two mouthfuls of hot beer and slammed the bottle. 'Is why we gat foh listen to all dis shit? Why you-all don't send John to de flipping mental? Whole day he smoking joint, and shooting shit! That man don't like de P.N.C. one damn! An he really believe is John de Baptist write Revelation.'

Another pork-knocker looked at Fieldor, and shrugged. 'He tink is easy, noh?' Then to the man. 'You don' just up and send a man to a madhouse, friend. You got full up a lot a paper with fancy questions. Why *you* don' try and send he if you tink is easy?'

Fieldor sniggered.

'Look, wha I mean,' said the accuser, 'is dis, people listenin' to he would tink black people always does bad-talk one another.'

'Don' worry wid dat! It tek a black man foh win a scholarship!' someone reminded, and the rest cried, 'cheers to dat!'

'Change you-all sinful ways!' advised the reformer, 'before Christ come and turn you-all into black shit-hounds.'

The gold-digger in the shop staggered to his feet, picked up an empty bottle and hurled it at the prophet in the dark, challenging, 'Turn dis into a shit-hound!' He didn't expect a hit, but the bottle landed true, opening the man's head. There ensued a barrage of profanity as the lunatic collapsed, but even grounded he continued to censure: 'Lord, Lord, forgive these lame shit-hounds.'

The minister chinked glasses with Serwall and Oscar, then looked for Rosita.

'She's gone in,' said Oscar.

The clergyman smiled, sipped his whisky, then beckoned with his glass. 'It's a shame, all that blasphemy!'

'Rather,' admitted Serwall, tilting badly in a chair, 'it's because they lacked the foundation.'

The next morning Rosita woke to find the villagers nailing up a banner across the road.

'Oscar! Oscar!' She nudged the sleeping figure, 'Look outside!'

'Huh?'

'Look,' she said, pointing excitedly.

'Well, I declare!' he muttered, a cheerful glow creeping into his red eyes.

A few men had painted WELCOME HOME on a long canvas, and were erecting it across the road. In smaller letters were written Danny Thorne – HERO. Bellying in the wind, the blue and white canvas looked impressive indeed.

'Danny boy,' said Roger.

'Why do you always say that?'

Roger shrugged. 'Reminds me of an Irish ballad. Tell me, how come you never showed me a photograph of Lily?'

'Well, an old Guyanese ballad says, "It bad medicine to show friend photograph of girlfriend, in case friend run off with her." '

They lunched at the Hotel Tower, belated celebrations to their success, but Danny was not particularly happy. Many incidents had upset his equilibrium. He had received bonuses from home for his impeccable performance, but it was news from home that had set his mind racing. As he examined the menu card, his thoughts dwelled on the contents of Oscar's letter,

Dear son,

'I hope by now you will have forgiven us for the necessary lie, but if we had told you the truth as to why Lily's marriage was cancelled, it might have messed up your entire career. I'm sure, you haven't regretted the decision I made years ago for, today, you've made history. Remember, I always said that whatever happens, happens for the best. Well, now you've gained everything when once everything looked hopeless. I trust this lesson will serve you well in the future. Rosita and I are expecting you this month end, only please be careful when travelling. I understand that racial disturbances in Georgetown and in some country areas have worsened. Avoid using public transport. If anything serious happens between now and month end, cancel your trip! Please don't get into political arguments, and avoid groups as far as possible.

'Do you remember how I respected your wishes when you begged to remain in town to study through your end-of-term holidays? Well, now it's my turn to ask a favour.

'Lily told Rosita she wrote you concerning a certain matter, and that since her letter, you haven't replied. I know it must have hurt to know the truth, and perhaps this is none of my business, but I can't ignore my conscience. Believe me, life is never a clean measure-and-cut affair. Had it not been for Lily's misfortune, today she'd be married to Dianand, and you'd always be haunted by memories of her. One thing I know – nothing has changed her love for you.

'I accept you reserve the right to decide for yourself the social implications of Lily's past, but we know she never loved anyone else, nor has she ever considered anyone, though many have written to Serwall asking for her hand – in spite of her past! She's a diamond, Danny, therefore, whatever you feel, let her know. The torture of your silence is worse for her. If my opinion means anything, a girl of Lily's integrity is worth ten of those professedly decent city girls. Anyway, what's pride when love is at stake?'

Oscar had closed with a reminder that Danny beware of discussions, keep early nights, and steer clear of crowds, et cetera.

He smiled at Oscar's concern but grew serious when he considered the advice proffered. He knew, somehow, Oscar was right, nonetheless, he couldn't ignore the hurt whenever he thought about Somir. About Lily being helpless in his filthy arms!

He knew her innocence, but God, why Somir! All these years, the girl he loved and respected – raped by his archenemy! He had been planning on his return to teach that rascal a lesson – now this! And what about his boast of the chaste girl he was going to marry? What when the truth surfaced?

'Hey, you're bending that spoon!' Roger warned.

'Wha – heavens!' Danny looked up in alarm. 'I – I wasn't thinking.'

'Boy, I'd say you *were*! Those must have been hysterical thoughts. You should've seen your mask a moment ago.'

Danny straightened himself. 'I'm sorry.'

Roger looked at him benignly. 'You've changed noticeably of late, and I'm sure it's not the scholarship. Want to talk about it?'

Danny looked thoughtful. 'Yes,' he nodded, 'it's true, I am upset, but I – I'm sorry, this is personal.' He clasped his hands and rested his chin on them.

'Okay. have it your way, but it's always best – to – get ...' Roger noticed his friend's disappointment, cleared his throat, and was silent throughout the meal.

However, soon as they were outside, Danny placed his hand around Roger's shoulder.

'I'm sorry about the bear treatment back there; you're too great a friend to lose. I hope you understand.'

Roger grinned and nodded.

Danny changed the subject as they paid the fare on entering a taxi-cab. 'It's getting too warm for comfort, here. Last week they nearly killed an Indian guy near my place. The thing is, that fellow is the least of the party apostles. He never even voted in his life.'

'Who'd know that?'

'But why? The politicians who start the trouble don't feel the squeeze. Meantime Blacks continue to harass Indians, and vice versa, without a clue what's going on.'

'The man on the rostrum rules the world,' said Roger.

At this, the taxi driver, a fat East Indian man with a walrus moustache, nodded like a bull. 'Bays, da ah true-true ting you-ah talk dey. Man, you-all talk like some Guiana schalars.' They shot each other secretive glances. The driver continued, 'Yoh mean foh say young man like you-all dis, know soh much, an beeg, beeg man like-ah meself does be so hignarant? Is a shame at de hignarance in dis country. Is still a country, noh? Or is ah calany?'

They got off near Lamaha Street, where they parted. Further down the road Danny heard a public address system atop a slow moving car blaring, 'Come one, come all, the P.N.C. will be holding a meeting tonight at the Bourda Green. Come and hear such speakers as ...' On and on the announcement trumpeted, even long after the car had crawled out of sight.

The next afternoon Danny chanced a stroll. The atmosphere in Georgetown wasn't really fraught with tension. At the corner of High and Croal Streets, outside the Magistrates' Court a group of men were articulating their views on the political situation. The media referred to these street-corner politicians as 'self-styled parliamentarians'. Arguments over their credibility and wisdom were invariably controversial. Danny tuned in to this episode.

'Look.' A tall, neatly dressed man with a felt hat, whom the others called Walter, raised a finger, and everyone inadvertently looked to the sky. 'I believe that the Portagee in this country ain't no better than any other race. They don't have unity among themselves. Owny the salt-good shop owners who meet from time to time does really correlate, odders does behave like they got a caste system. You don't have to investigate to know that the Portagees in good jobs snob them who live in Albuoystown, and the former, in turn, is snobbed by the high-brows ...'

'Wha is a high-brow?' whispered one man.

'Ah rich man wha does walk like a king, with he eyebrows pull back,' informed another, showing disappointment at his friend's ignorance.

'... You ever see twenty Portagee of different social calibre get together foh defend one another? Never!' The speaker shook his head, 'but look at black man! In no time a hundred of them jumping in the mêlée foh defend their mattee black man, whether he right or wrong ... Who say black man ain't got unity? That ain't true, eh?'

Danny pretended at tying his shoelace. The men surrounding Walter thought for a while, then, one by one, heads began to bob. Then a chant of 'Is true, Walter talking good,' went up.

The self-appointed chairman proceeded. 'Now, the P.P.P. in power, and any fool know that they have the majority, right? Right?' He waited for their nods before continuing, 'It is also true that the P.N.C. would have to produce a miracle to snatch the cup from the P.P.P.'s hand ...' The gathering sniggered at Walter's play upon words, for the cup was the P.P.C.'s political symbol.

'Look.' Again he raised his hand, and several misguided heads turned to see. The eloquent Walter was standing high, extremely dignified. 'The P.N.C. can only secure votes from negroes, therefore, ...'

A violent outburst ended further speculations.

'Walter!' they thundered, 'you gone back with dat shit!

100

How de piss you know owny black man does vote foh de Palm Tree?'

The others who had been listening with rapt attention cut loose vehemently. 'Look, Walter, we been putting up wid you bullshit too long! If you can't talk proper – shut your ass!'

The speaker looked so disillusioned Danny had to stifle a laugh. He walked off, the hum-drum of the men echoing in his ears, drowning Walter's protests of 'Ow, man, I ain't mean the one one East Indian and Portagee who does vote foh the Palm Tree. ...'

Danny went to his desk, sat down, put his hands to his temples, and wondered how race relations could turn so sour. He recalled that in the orphanage, 'race' was indicated by name; Sampson meant Black, Gomes – Portuguese, Singh – East Indian, and so forth. It never went beyond that. Significant was that orphans sided with orphans; anyone outside the orphanage was a non-orphan and, therefore, not of the fraternity.

For the nuns two categories sufficed, the Holies, and the Holy Terrors. That anyone harboured racial hatred was unthinkable! True, there were times of late when he felt extreme contempt for those whites in South Africa who reportedly treated Blacks worse than dirt, and he often questioned his friendship with Roger, but Roger had been more of a friend to him than had many Blacks!

Admittedly there were white boys at college who kept aloof and appeared to consider themselves superior, but there were also those mulattoes who didn't mingle with anyone! The sons of Pakistani businessmen, Danny noticed, moved with a marked air of detachment and a distinction between East Indian lads of different castes was obvious. And what of Jessel? Jessel the Jew who was always respectful to everyone? Did he feel inferior? Was it because, as Danny sadly observed, the college hierarchy held little respect for the sympathetic or the friendly?

Then there were the slogans of the East Indians which angered and hurt him bitterly. Was it true that Blacks were hopeless at business, poor decision makers, 'naturally destructive' people? Was that why he, Danny, with all his heart wanted to be Somir's executioner?

No! It was Somir who was the pagan! Was he, Danny, to do nothing while Somir raped Lily and went scot free? Lily said she no longer despised Somir – well, maybe her powers of forgiveness were extraordinary, and he respected her for that – but his hurt was too great. All those years of discipline couldn't repress one moment of steaming hate.

Suddenly he found himself praying – the legacy bequeathed to him by the nuns. Their method of self-correction. *You* prayed for those who cuffed the daylights out of you. *You* asked God's forgiveness if you felt one drop of enmity. But Danny knew it: once the heart went foul, the mind drank bilge-water. In spite of himself, he smiled, opened a drawer and took out Lily's envelope. He then proceeded with the more pleasant task of re-reading her letter, corking his ears with his thumbs.

'My dearest Danny,

'I have not seen you in five years, seven months, one week and six days, yet I hold you in my heart as one I had kissed only yesterday, more so now the time for your return draws near. With all that is in me, I regret what happened, but painful memories die with us – no matter our efforts to the contrary – and we can only but try to live with them. My ill-fortune could have been anyone's – try to remember that. I write this, possibly my last letter, in the hope you will understand how I feel. At first I was bitter, too bitter to write even to you (as you may remember) but prayer helped me.

'Of course, I'm ashamed, but I no longer despise Somir, for I've grown to understand that the mischief goes beyond his thoughts. He was never the recipient of parental love, or guidance, and if anyone is to judge in this, it is God alone.

'All I am asking is that you find it in your heart to forgive me, the victim, for I can never explain what I felt in my moment of hopelessness. Were it not for Rosita, I don't know what would have become of me. Her kindness and instructions were crutches I needed desperately. I am now old enough to understand many things, foremost being the nature of a person, and I know it was because of your mild nature that I first loved you. As we would love Christ, whatever He be, for His immaculate nature.

'If you feel my past is too wicked to accept, I shall try to see with you. I am not begging, it's just that I can't bear to lose you. My love will never change, only I don't know why fate had to choose this stigma for me.'

At this point the handwriting scrawled. Danny's nausea sprang from guilt. For a moment, a feeling rushed upon him, and he knew, if she were there, he would have taken her in his arms, and comforted, 'Don't worry, darling, I'll never leave you – *never*!'

Rosita undid her apron, opened the back door, and went downstairs to empty the trash bin. On the verge of executing this chore she staggered back, screaming. Oscar dashed out through the back door to find Rosita trembling, metres from the pit, her hands clutching her mouth. Soon he, too, was staring in horror, for there, amid the rinds, cans, and stuff, lay Paddy, his head severed, his superficial grin covered with flies.

'God!' cried Oscar, stepping back involuntarily.

Rosita was hysterical.

'Only a maniac would do this!'

'Who, Oscar, could have the heart to …?' She cried.

'Go on upstairs,' he advised, then took her arm, for, indeed, she seemed unable to move.

Later, he sought out the sergeant. The lawman sighed, but slowly, his eyes began to fire calculating glances at the forest, at Oscar. 'It's beginning to add up,' he said finally.

'What?'

'Everything. The children's bogeyman; the disappearance, of clothing, food … now this! It's obviously the work of Somir.'

'Somir!' Oscar turned to face the rows of trees over to the east.' So he's still alive. How can anyone live like that … after all these years?'

'Anyone sane, you mean.'

'What are you going to do?'

'I have something of a plan.'

'Can I help?'

'Yes and no. I've been talking to Sam – you know he and Somir were friends – and he feels that when Danny returns, Somir is going to reveal himself …'

'I hope you're not planning to use Danny for bait!'

'Of course not! I'd like to suggest that when he arrives, everyone in your house spend that night with Ben. Just leave your house empty.'

Oscar pondered. 'Do you think Somir will fall for it?'

'I'm sure he will. I only hope he doesn't have a bomb,' Hopkinson smiled, 'because I'll be in the house – waiting.'

'Am I to assume then, that the killing of Paddy … that there's method in madness?'

'Exactly, and Paddy, I fear, is only the beginning.'

Oscar breathed hard. 'Can't we do anything now?'

'Well, we can get together another search party. You know what happened before? No. I'll warn everyone again to keep a sharp eye on the kids. One has to take Somir seriously. Anyway, I'm going to make a final search. See if I can spot anything. Wish me luck.'

'Okay, Hoppy.'

When the lawman had gone, Oscar eyed the forest prophetically. After all these years, no one could be the same … not living in there!

It was drizzling when Oscar picked up a spade, dug a hole and buried Paddy. He was erecting a little wooden cross when Sergeant Hopkinson appeared from behind the hibiscus hedge, his handkerchief working briskly over his head and face.

'Hell, man! You nearly scared the stuffing out of me! Where've you been? Look at your clothes!'

'In there,' Hopkinson indicated the forest, 'and there's no doubt, Somir's our man. I found the remains of a fire. It doesn't look good. From the footprints, I'd say he walks in circles. I followed some tracks that led to the river. He could have crossed, I'm not sure, but look, near the fire, I found this.' He handed over three crumpled pages from an exercise book.

'Let's go under the house,' advised Oscar, 'this drizzle's getting worse.'

Oscar examined the drawings. They looked like the sketches of a six-year old, but all were signed 'Somir.'

'I don't understand.'

'Look at the back of this page.'

Oscar read:

'I, the undersine, herby athorise you, Mr Banker, for pay the bearer, Daniel, the sum of 1000 Dollar for the bearer's finiral. Then notetify me about farder tansactions. And kill off dem beggars outside de bank, they're Molesk my Custimer. Send sweets for me wife, Lily, and stop sending me messages about Daniel. Stop it you bastads! Hes only a nigger! Dont forget the sweets. She is *my* wife.

POEM
'Sweet and swat,
Butter and fat,
Tonite I gwan kill,
A big, fluffly cat.'

Oscar looked at the sergeant. 'Already I feel sorry for him. He's quite mad!'

Hopkinson scratched his head. 'Tell me something I don't know.'

'What now?'

'Think I'll go and warn the people.'

The burly lawman took the pages, stuffed them into his shirt pocket, and left.

Oscar watched him make his exit through the gate, through the rain. He glanced at the tiny cross near the flamboyant tree. What did Paddy have to do with it?

Sam walked slowly along the length of the creek with his son in his arms. A monarch butterfly flitted over the yellow daisy flowers like a coloured wrapper tossed about in the wind.

'Look, butterfly! See? Butterfly.' Sam pointed, and lightly jogged the small child in his arms.

The boy gazed with bright black eyes wherever Sam pointed, and hugged his father tightly around the neck.

'Look, look! Birdies, bir-dy!'

Big innocent eyes looked up to see several egrets flying by and two chubby hands went up excitedly.

'Da-da! Da-da!'

Sam took an almighty breath and looked at his son with profound satisfaction.

As he rambled back to the village, fondling and teasing his child along the way, he wondered if Sergeant Hopkinson wasn't getting worked up unnecessarily. Could Somir find it in his heart to harm a baby? A baby as sweet at this one? He doubted it, but just in case Somir made an ass of himself, the axe Sam used to chop firewood would speak.

Lily sat, fingers fidgeting in her lap, listening to the sermon. Every so often Rosita would glance at her. The service was well attended.

The minister had a habit of using his spectacles like a baton for emphasis. That morning histrionics got the better of him, and while he was 'whipping the thieves outside the temple,' his spectacles went flying across the congregation. This was promptly greeted with laughter. The altar boy hurried after the missile, walked proudly back up the aisle, and returned it to the embarrassed clergyman, one lens missing.

On their way home Rosita tried to get through to Lily.

'Our minister is funny, did you see his face?' she chuckled.

'Yes.'

'Oh, Lily, you didn't as much as smile.'

'I – I'm not feeling up to it these days.' She tucked her handbag under her arm agitatedly.

'Don't worry,' Rosita said, 'he'll write. I know he will.'

'Will he? I feel so – so depressed. Oh, Rosita, am I going to end up like father?'

'Your dad's all right! Anyway, you shouldn't question

the wisdom of God. This is His way … You must accept your cross.'

'Yes, I know! It's just that it doesn't seem right!' Her eyes started to water. Rosita placed an arm around her. 'Don't think about it, dear. Just don't think about it.'

While the people looted and burned; while stray bullets found a few innocent bystanders; while would-be saboteurs roamed alleyways armed with Molotov cocktails, or fragmentation bombs – Danny Thorne sat writing a letter. For four consecutive nights he had not slept. Had been unable to ignore the things feeding on his conscience. One of the largest industrial companies had offered him an engineering scholarship, and civil disturbances threatened the land – it was enough to keep anyone's mind active. Yet, he couldn't forget her. He was hounded by the excitement that, soon, he would come face to face with her, he would be able to hold and kiss the girl whose love overpowered him. He recalled his departure from Mahdia, how his heart had bled during that long, agonising trip.

Nearly six years ago, and yet it was as if he could touch that terrible memory, and the more he wrote, the more he yearned to be with her. He mentioned that dark evening when they stole down to the creek; when he was too shy to hold her hand; when a frog leaped into the water and they grabbed at each other.

He smiled, recalling her alarm, how *he* had jumped. Yes, he loved her. For moments he recaptured her girlish smile, and he closed his eyes. God! In a fit of temper he pounded the desk. If only Somir were dead! Why couldn't they find him? Was he dead? Frustration devoured him, that a rapist should be allowed to roam freely.

Danny's expression grew cold when he remembered Somir. The day they beat him into the dust and almost shattered his faith in the human race – he hadn't forgotten Somir's victorious grin. Unconsciously he flexed his muscles. There was no doubt in his mind. Somir had better be prepared!

Reports of Danny's success as a Guiana scholar were pouring in. His name was broadcast over and again. 'Danny Thorne of Mahdia' was becoming a national hero!

Somir gulped mouthfuls of rum, grimaced, then belched as he leaned back. So, Danny was returning – for Lily! He kicked the transistor so viciously it flew into the air, hit a tree and went dead. Somir bit his lip hard. He was forced to live like a beast while a nigger was glorified! Tears lingered in his eyes. He had to eat frogs and mouldy bread while Danny had the best, and now he wanted Lily too!

Slowly he grasped an object in his satchel. In the moonlight a steel blade glinted. Sniffing, Somir got up. He swore aloud and began to stab repeatedly at a nearby tree. Anyone seeing him would have conceded that he looked stark, raving mad.

10

The news of Danny's homecoming set everyone bustling with activity. Children went to great pains to shout greetings at everyone they could lay hands on; wives baked custards and extravagant cakes and had men throwing up their heads and sniffing with loud 'aah's'; from Sister Baldeo's quarters the poignant aroma of black-pudding augered well for the spree ahead and cronies convened to scrub and adorn the church altar with fresh flowers from Ben's garden. However, tranquillity was the order of the day, except for those over-anxious well-wishers who had erected the WELCOME HOME banner prematurely, and had to take it down for repairs and another coat of paint.

Rosita surprised everyone with her agility when she chased a fowl to near exhaustion. But while Lily curled up her toes and read Danny's letter and – depending on the tone – smiled or cried with the gusto of a child; while Serwall had become himself again, 'strengthened' by the knowledge that his 'baby' would be married to a brilliant scholar for whose foundation he could take full credit; while pork-knockers dropped their warishis, made grand speeches with words no one had ever heard before, and banged bottles, and boasted how Mahdia was untouched by racism; while people marvelled at the quantity of liquor Oscar consumed, Somir sat on the high root of a giant mora, deep in the jungle, eating a half-roasted snake with lunatic urgency. Suddenly, he became still, not chewing, and raised his eyes under low brows to stare ahead like a man possessed.

Danny walked over the window to gaze upon the Promenade. For years he had looked through this window, thinking about home, about Lily. Schoolboys were climbing gnarled-buttressed ficus trees on the western end of the ground, playing at Tarzan. He heard the very popular militia band softly blowing folk songs to a fair-sized, appreciative audience.

Sometimes they played selections from Tchaikovsky and Chopin, flooding Danny with nostalgia, framing pictures of the wild fauna, the dark, mysterious jungles, the roaring, foaming rapids of the Potaro, and his own silent, colossal mountains.

Those soul-warming classics forever awakened deep, cherished memories of Lily standing on the hill, her long hair wafting in the wind, and he would close his eyes and try to comprehend those fingers of elation clawing within, arousing every fibre in his tall, slender body.

Over the tree tops, over the bandstand and out of sight, in V formation, lending peace to the afternoon, flew a string of herons, their long, slender wings undulating rhythmically, transporting them like a silent squadron on some secret mission.

Many a day he studied there, on the Promenade, or enjoyed a novel, sitting on one of the many white, elaborately designed iron benches, sometimes rolling the cold pebbles under his bare feet, feeling closer to nature; sometimes watching the children play hide-and-seek in, under, and around the bandstand. He always noticed that when the youngest child was the seeker, and was unable to find anyone, he would glance around with big, forsaken eyes, and burst into tears, when the bigger lads would have to rush out to console him.

Often the surrounding beauty ensnared him, leaving him lost in admiration of the thickly petalled red and white roses that grew in countless arrangements, inhaling their perfume. Sometimes he would take off his shirt and stretch out on the lawn, fascinated by the hummingbirds fencing at multi-coloured masquerades – floribunda roses – for nectar, their little bodies stationary, the rapidity of their wings a pleasant test to the naked eye.

Cat's tail – red as any but a cat's – hung from large earthenware pots and below, in drums cut lengthways, bloomed the most exotic chrysanthemums, dahlias and morning glory bushes. The gloriosa superba, with its perianth leaves so delightfully flinted and scalloped, never failed to excite sensibility.

Near the side gate towered the majestic, golden candle-bush. Ladybirds, even those with red polka dots on black coats, patrolled every stem.

This one-block Eden, with its comb and brush flowers, and 'forbidden fruits' of the cannonball trees; its mammee trees with roundish, edible, russet fruits for which many a gallant climber got the hiding of his life; its lofty, gurgling fountain; its red, pebbled walks and thick, green lawns, brought solace to many.

Danny heard the children's voices behind the hibiscus. He could never understand why, when they played bat and ball, a good, lusty hit over the trees, over the road, smashing a window pane, was invariably 'six, and out'; or why 'Tarzan' usually lost face and cried when his playmates left him stranded in a high tree they dared him to climb, and ran away laughing.

He pulled out his suitcase and started to pack. Gunpat, an obliging boy from the household, came upstairs noiselessly and, finding the door ajar, pushed it, and peeped in.

'I can come in?'

'Yes, Guns, come in.'

Gunpat's fallen countenance told the story. Before, knowing Danny's appetite for knowledge, Gunpat was wont to ask those questions that break up friendships. Today his taciturnity was unparalleled. Danny tried to get him involved in the packing, but his presence filled the room with melancholy. Then a car horn sounded outside. Gunpat rushed to the window.

'It's Roger,' he mumbled, looking very unhappy indeed.

'Now, Guns, you're not going to start that! No long faces, remember? Anyway, I'll be back in town in less than a month. Look, be a sport; tell Roger I'll be down shortly.' Gunpat left the room reluctantly.

'Put the luggage in the back seat,' Roger advised Danny as he approached the car, 'the boot's dirty.'

'Those people actually look sorry to see you go.' Roger

waved back at the Indian trio waving broadly from a window.

Danny grinned. 'It's difficult not to like this nigger.'

'Accepted!' Roger put the Vauxhall into gear.

Three heads were still craning through the window when the car turned the corner.

When they reached the Georgetown stelling, instead of dropping him off, Roger drove down into the ferry lane.

'Hey, what you think you're doing?'

'You think I'll let you waste time hunting for a hire car when you get to Vreed-en-hoop?'

'Well, I was hoping to catch the train.'

'What, and get lovesick on that romantic journey? Oh, no! Besides your Oscar would catch a fit!

'Really, man, I hope you're not putting yourself out?'

'For you? Who do you think you are?'

As usual the ferry crossing was tiring. The vessel laboured across the Demerara, churning the heavy brown water into a foamy mass. Up the river, near the fishing pens, seagulls piped contentedly to discarded fish. Sometimes they floated with the steady current, extremely still, like rubber ducks.

The sun was a bloody football behind the velvety green of the Essequibo. Here and there in the eddying wake of the ferry, fishes played, their white bellies contrasting with the reddish water. Who would have dreamt that the very next day not two hundred metres away, the Sun Chapman with its human cargo bound for Wismar would sail its last voyage? An eye-witness said the explosion ripped the ferry apart like a match-box.

At last the Makouria neared the stelling and the sailors, looking smart in their navy-blue uniforms and white embroidered collars, burst into activity, throwing ropes with delightful accuracy to men on landings, shouting instructions, exchanging taunts, and laughing. The faithful vessel was finally moored.

Roger's car led the way since it was the last aboard, and they drove out at a snail's pace – the metal gangway banging and clanging deafeningly under the weight of the vehicle.

A child ran down the stelling with a sickly-looking catfish dangling on a hook, shouting, 'Small Boy, Small Boy, watch wha I ketch,' while the assistant harbour master implored him to keep off the premises.

'Hey!' cried Roger, pointing. 'Watermelon!'

The corpulent Indian vendor smiled invitingly at Roger as she cut the melon, but every so often she glanced at his companion with expressionless eyes. As they ate the succulent fruit, its delicious red juice running down their hands, Roger remarked, 'I still can't figure out how you cleared those distinctions – with the eighty-day strike and all.'

'See the fading circles under my eyes,' Danny said, his mouth full, the words slurring. 'You didn't do too badly yourself, for a playboy!'

Wiping sticky hands and forearms furiously, sweet and fruit vendors imploring them to 'buy something, nuh, betta,' they chatted freely. Just as the car was about to move off, a sot staggered up to Danny's window, spittle hanging from his chin on to the car door, his eyes almost closed.

'You-all niggers! Ah-we coolie gon brock ah-you rass.'

Roger pulled off, leaving the man like the leaning tower.

'Did he get to you?'

'Naw, he's too drunk.'

'I'd have liked to see Lily, really,' Roger said, 'but my parents won't permit it. Say it's too risky.'

'I agree. Especially now.'

'Mom gets nervy if I say I'm going out-of-town.' Danny smiled, 'Mothers are fussy. Rosita is the same. As for Oscar – don't do this, don't use public transport – they must think I'm still twelve!'

'You believe things'll get worse?' Roger asked.

'I hope not.'

'Boy, so many houses already razed to the ground.'

Roger honked a few times, the driver ahead signalled him on, and he accelerated, the engine screaming as he overtook the lorry, two Morris Oxfords, a blue wooden bus, then negotiated a wide, smooth turn, while the grass alongside the road whipped the metal fender.

'That Abraham disaster took the cake,' Roger continued. 'I'd like to know what makes such a guy tick. I mean, to roast six children and their parents in the dead of night – it's ghastly!'

Danny remained silent, and struggled with his thoughts about Somir. Was it people like him who were responsible for these disasters? Oscar and even Lily had made excuses for him. But if Somir wasn't to be blamed, who was?

The tyres screeched on a sharp turn, and several cattle egrets took to wing. Before them lay a two mile stretch of asphalted road; they could see vapour rising. Roger accepted the silent challenge. Behind the car, composed of dust, smoke and pebbles, trailed a tornado.

A milkman on a fenderless bicycle, a Raleigh old enough to be considered a relic, swerved off the road in panic, then tried to stop the bike with his foot. He didn't succeed, and he, the bike, and the milk cans, ended up in a reed-filled canal.

A marabunta smashed against the windscreen. Six coconut palms in a row pirouetted by, and a woman with a sombrero-looking basket on her head, flew past, as did a dignified mother duck and four all-in-a-line peeping ducklings. A lad on a donkey waved, then he, too, rocketed past. They overtook a motorcyclist whose machine sounded worse than an asthmatic lorry, and he was soon diminishing behind them.

The wind pressed Danny's hair sideways, and flattened his cheek. He gripped the dashboard, and his shoes mashed at non-existent brakes.

'Have you decided which university to go to?' Roger shouted above the noise of the engine.

'Not yet. Maybe your dad can advise me.'

'Sure. Now that he's decided to return to England, we'll be able to see each other when you arrive. When do you expect to fly?'

'At the speed you're going, in a very short while!'

Roger grinned and eased his foot off the pedal. The engine fell to an even hum.

'Okay?'

Danny stretched back in the spacious seat, blowing.
'Cool, man, cool.'

He slipped a mint into his mouth, flicked the wrapper out of the car, and inhaled the fresh wind rushing over the coastland. Once more, his thoughts strayed to Mahdia. He was actually bridging six years with this trip!

They drove along a sea of sugar cane, tall, with golden plumes undulating dreamily in the sunshine. Beyond the open fields, behind a tumbledown mudhouse, a tiny train toiled, black smoke issuing from its stack.

'Imagine,' Roger said, beckoning at the vast land, 'One man to dictate all this.'

The car slowed to crawl over a humped bridge, and they saw wattled jacanas stepping daintily along the soft canal mud. A young man, trying in all earnest to 'stick' on a bicycle, received an ovation from his friends when he collapsed on the parapet and, obviously, hurt his ankle.

Sometimes a pretty, auburn-skinned girl would return Roger's salutation, though many looked shy, or giggled. At Roger's insistence Danny waved at one, but received a sour glance.

'Just testing,' said Roger.

'I could have told you,' Danny said.

Finally they arrived in Parika, the mouth of the Essesquibo. Newspaper boys shouted headlines and fanned papers to the sky. Trays were stacked with succulent fruits. They parked, and deposited Danny's luggage on the quay, while vendors flocked around them beseechingly.

'Ow, Bet, buy something, nuh?'

One smiled, displaying thirty-two gold teeth and said, 'This banana full-ah sugar, love, buy ah dallah; nuh? Hey, try wan.'

Danny, an overnight bag slung over his shoulder, purchased a very heavy pineapple. The woman made the sale without supplication. Roger said it appeared she lost in the transaction. Danny chuckled.

'Here, this is for your mom.'

'Boy, this is a whopper! She'll love it, thanks.'

'Tell her I'll miss her cottage-pies.'

'Take care of yourself,' Roger said, and they shook

hands. The ferry was boarded by a crowd that, as usual, shoved, leaned, burrowed, and moaned. Roger perpetually criticised this inability to queue, but Danny would counter with 'No one can criticise better than a foreigner.'

Danny squeezed his way to the side rail, almost slipping on a mango rind.

'Thanks again,' he shouted.

'I'll drop you a line,' Roger promised.

'Don't forget; keep your eyes on the road!'

'Don't worry. Have a smashing trip, and let us know how love's blooming.'

The caterpillar in the oil-blackened engine-room started to hum, and below the stern the water began to eddy no rougher than the circles a paddle creates in still water, then to churn and foam savagely as the engine rose to a deafening crescendo. The propeller whipped the water into white froth then sprayed it back uniformly upon the river's face.

The vessel parted from the stout greenheart stelling. Roger stood, legs astride, smiling, waving both hands overhead, his hair like Oscar's, all over his face.

A little Indian boy nudged his way up to the rail, looked up at Danny, then to Roger, and captivated by the farewell excitement, began to jump up and down, and call enthusiastically. Danny smiled down at the innocent heart, unbridled by prejudices. One that saw a friend in every stranger.

He watched Roger walk to the car. Seconds later, thin smoke trailed from the exhaust, and the vehicle moved off. Danny remembered the mints in his pocket, and looked around for the child, but its mother had pulled it roughly away.

Four men played rap in a passage-way on the floor, and those wishing to pass had to step over. In another group a man was telling an English botanist about the bushmaster. How the bite of this snake was 'baaad!'

'Is it fatal?' asked the bearded foreigner, to which the man smiled in amusement that this big university scholar didn't know the bushmaster.

'When he bite you, friend, you got exactly one minute foh live!'

An ordinary-looking farmer with a sweat-stained felt hat said, 'I ain sure 'bout dat, but ah know if you ain get medical 'tention quick, you gone foh channa.'

'Gone foh channa?' The foreigner's chin dropped.

'He mean you cork duck,' said the first.

'Oh,' The man smiled, assuming that the gibberish had started.

The ferry travelled down-river for hours. Danny stood watching scores of insects floating past in the sun-reflected water. Soon he collided with nostalgia. Blessed memory, how well he remembered Mahdia! And how close he felt to the girl he loved. He leaned on the wooden rail staring into the rushing, swirling river, the bubbles, the froth, saw an occasional floating box, or vegetable, then, as though in a vision the river became blushing sands rolling by and in it he discerned Lily. He saw deeper into the river, and everything died. Arabesque patterns appeared, his soul and the swishing water, the black-striped fishes, the strong odours of diesel and grease, were one gigantic force.

He became vaguely aware of the monotonous humming, that they were moving. The breeze had grown chilly. They passed scores of islands, crude stellings, landings, and hundreds of noisy birds, but he paid them little attention. He was conscious only of foam, water, and the salty spray touching his cheek.

His muscles twitched, his skin grew. Again the boat lifted and plunged. Again the spray danced in the air. Cries of 'Oooh,' went up along the rail and a few jumped back. Danny smiled inwardly.

Finally the river narrowed; the water was lighter in colour. The savage battle-cry of a kiskadee pierced the droning of the engine, and the botanist resumed his conversation.

'What about the labara?' he asked

'De wha?' The men screwed up their faces.

'The labara. Isn't there such a snake?'

'Oh, you muss mean de labaria!'

117

'The labaria? Yes, that's it!' confessed the foreigner.

'Well, dat,' informed the first, 'is a real baad customer. Man, he baad like soor.' He nodded portentously, leaving the foreigner to ponder whether 'baad' meant less venomous than 'baaad'. A 'bad' snake obviously wasn't too deadly. But what did 'soor' mean? Something as evil as the labaria, no doubt!

On the deck, those standing at the rail shifted from one foot to the other, or peeled tangerines and ate, or sighed. Others paced the deck tirelessly, or read newspapers, or snored on a bench. Youths 'tackled' girls who giggled at all overtures to their girl friends, who giggled encouragingly.

A young man strummed a guitar tunelessly over in a rope-infested corner, much to the frustration of an Indian lad wearing a silken red shirt, and moss-green jeans. He got up, walked over to the soloist and asked, 'You can play "The Green, Green, Grass of Home?"' He received a pause, a broken-toothed grin, a brisk nod, and immediately the guitarist began what certainly seemed like the requested tune, but minutes later, it trailed back into the previously calamitous composition.

So absorbed in a monumental paperback was one man, others suspected it was a sex-crammed work, but when the Englishman, perhaps suspicious of the local definitions of venom, took out a similar volume to read, those very souls gazed respectfully for, undoubtedly, his book was heavy stuff.

Sergeant Hopkinson lifted the bonnet, screwed off the rusting radiator cap, and filled the tank with water. Lily skipped out of the house the moment she spotted him. He was shining the manufacturer's emblem when she came up.

'Everything okay?'

'Yes, yes, yes, young lady,' he smiled, 'so stop worrying. I'm going to bring back your sweetheart without a scratch.'

Lily experienced a cold shiver of felicity at 'sweetheart'. She flushed.

118

'All right, but make sure you have sufficient petrol.'

'Madam,' he invited, with a little bow and a delicate sweep of the hand towards the jeep, 'would you care to....'

While they chatted freely, two boys with an air rifle stood near the parlour on the lookout for a moving target. It was a powerful gun but neither had ever shot a bird in flight, and such a shortcoming always left a question mark over one's marksmanship. Since Oscar had killed the ocelot, hunting had become a craze. The boys were only a few minutes waiting when a large flock of birds came into sight, flying over the village, right over them! And so low! His hands trembling, the older lad took aim – at what he wasn't sure – and fired. There was some commotion in the flock, then, to the utter delight of the hunter, one of the birds plummeted to the ground.

Lily, who was standing in the path of the bird's death fall, had her dress sprinkled with blood. She leapt back as the egret landed at her feet, shot through the neck. On the ground it struggled immensely, scratching up the dust, fluttering out its life.

'Better go rinse that right away,' advised the sergeant.

The youngsters rushed to inspect the kill, and the smaller boy flew into a rage when he saw where the pellet had struck.

'Fluke!' he screamed, and remonstrated bitterly.

The sergeant seeing the marksman's predicament, intervened. 'I think it was a true and perfect shot, son. Davy Crockett couldn't have done better.'

Lily scrubbed the blood with all her might, but there still remained finger-spot stains. She considered burning the dress. She was terribly upset by the incident, and the clipping noise of the bird's beak, the red-stained feathers, the spurting blood, and the dust, reminded her of something she would rather have forgotten. She tried to interpret this 'omen', for of late she had become surprisingly superstitious. But while she racked her brains for an answer, her subconscious collected the day's events, dumped them into a knapsack, and sat waiting to go on a midnight safari.

At prayers that evening she gave special thanks for Danny's return – admitting that the heartaches had been worth it – and soon fell into a contented sleep.

Two hours later she found herself in a desolate land, crowded with strange trees, all of a sinister hue, even the leaves, which hung like old, wrinkled ears, and from their midst burst a flock of birds with gargantuan, misshapen beaks that clapped deafeningly. Large as pelicans, the featherless creatures were running straight at her. She tried to scream, but couldn't. She tried to run, but her feet were stuck to the earth. And the enormous birds, mud caked to their bodies, their plucked, lifeless necks dangling, bore down on her, trotting to the rhythm of the beaks. They were almost upon her when blood started to spill from their eyes, nostrils, and beaks, and their naked wings started to beat. She screamed, covering her ears, as one bird opened its beak wider than a hippo's mouth and threatened to swallow her up … She sprang up in a paroxysm of terror, gasping, but the ungodly monsters were safely imprisoned behind those mysterious gates.

11

It wasn't long before the children established a 'Mahdia Patrol'. Every day they gathered outside Fieldor's parlour, and proceeded through the village. Usually they returned, lathered in perspiration to announce to the relief of poultry rearers, 'No thefts! All's well on the Mahdia front!'

One day, however, they reported, 'One fowl stolen from Mr Jack Tyre, the foreign liar!' and parent rushed out in alarm, hushing them. They considered it rude to label the American a liar, though this was the general opinion.

Jack had come to British Guiana eight years ago to prospect, and made a strike on his first outing. Then his luck petered out and now he found himself struggling with a kitchen garden in Mahdia. Vanity and conceit constantly nagged him, and he refused to be put down as a Yankee eking out an existence in a remote corner of a relatively unknown land in South America, so he circulated the story that he was a millionaire visiting for reasons of health. The climate, he said, was ideal for his condition. But what condition exactly, nobody knew.

John was first to notice the feathers. He surfaced in the middle of the creek, and felt them, clammy on his face. At first he thought they came from above, but then more came floating down.

'Hey, you two!' he called, 'see whey dem feathers coming from.'

They investigated.

'Is fowl feathers,' they hailed.

He joined them. 'Ah can see is fowl feathers, you ass, ah say see whey dey comin from.'

Twenty metres up the creek, behind a clump of reeds on the opposite bank they discovered the bogeyman, a half-plucked chicken in one hand, a saucepan in the other. Immediately they began to stone him.

'Fetch the sergeant,' ordered John, and the smallest snatched up his pants and bolted.

But nothing materialised from the encounter, for the sergeant and Oscar had gone for Danny, and nobody seemed anxious to venture into a sweltering jungle after a heavy lunch. Nevertheless, the daredevils swore that stones had opened the bogey's head, that they had him 'runnin foh he life,' so the villagers silently sympathised with the rapist and forgot the matter.

Not surprisingly, the narrative told among contemporaries was of a more dramatic nature. Now it was they who were ambushed by a madman with a sword. They who had to slip that razor-sharp blade like karate experts. They who had to fight – how their little hands demonstrated! – to overpower him. They who ... And Superman looked down upon the planet Tazap whose inhabitants never quarrelled, nor sighed, nor hated, nor worried, and wondered if he couldn't play the villain just for once, and zap them with a fire beam.

Lily dried, wrapped the towel about herself, and stepped out of the bathroom. Then she brushed her hair, pleased with the waves, the healthy shine. Her breasts were firm against the towel and, she had noticed, a bit larger. She smiled as she hand-smoothed a ripple of hair. It was so soft! She made to move, when a reflection in the mirror caused her to turn sharply. The towel barely covered her decently. 'Daddy! What are you doing?'

'I – I wanted a safety-pin.'

'Why didn't you ... Never mind!' she fumed, but she wanted to demand why he had sneaked up on her. She handed over a pin from behind the door.

'You – you going somewhere?'

'Yes. On the hill for some fresh air. It's a bit stuffy in here!'

'You think it's safe?'

'I don't know what's safe these days!'

He cleared his throat. 'It's just that – that Oscar and I discussed your safety, your going about unprotected. We think you should avoid lonely spots.'

'Look, I think you're all making a mountain out of nothing. Somebody killed Sugars, and it certainly wasn't Somir. Why hasn't the murderer been found? Somir might be guilty of stealing, yes, but he's mad – everyone knows that.'

'Stealing's not all he's guilty of,' he reminded her.

'Okay, daddy, pour it in!' Anger flared up within her.

'I – I'm sorry. I didn't mean it that way.' He bowed and walked off.

She closed the door, dressed, and felt a lot more cheerful after she began to hum 'Suhanne raat' in her fine, melodious voice. She was opening the door when he confronted her.

'I – I think I ought to tell you ... I was admiring you back there.'

Lily's brow knitted, and her eyes demanded an explanation, but Serwall continued to regard her as if seeing her for the first time.

Then, in fond tones, he said, 'You've grown to look just like your mother. One day you'll have children of your own, and you'll understand why I've seemed such a miserable father. I – I was lonely and very unhappy for many years. This may have spoiled my judgement of – of many things. When I attempted to take my life it was because I was too selfish to realise how it could have damaged you. Just now, when I saw you looking so much like a woman, I couldn't believe my eyes. It's nothing, though, just ignore me, I'm growing old and sentimental, and afraid of losing you. But I know the time is fast approaching when you'll be wed ... and gone.' He looked away. 'The times I flogged you to ensure you avoided the pitfalls in life. I – I realise, now, how conceited and stupid I was. Can you forgive me, Lily?'

She held his arm. It felt soft, and frail.

'Yes, I believe I understand. Thank you, daddy. And don't worry, my marriage will not be our goodbye. You'll have grandchildren to keep you busy.'

Outside, closing the door quietly, she tiptoed lightheartedly down the stairs. Inside, Serwall picked up the photograph of Sati, sat down in the rocking chair, and shook his head sorrowfully, and sobs, founded in grief, rushed up, choking him.

Rosita was cobwebbing when Lily entered the room.

'Hi, I'm just doing some last-minute tidying.'

'His room looks new!'

'Must be the blinds,' suggested Rosita, dusting stuff off the sheets.

'Yes, they're gorgeous!'

'I hope he likes them half as much as he likes you.'

Lily smiled graciously. 'Here, I brought you my knitting needles.'

'Ah, you're a darling, but Peter will get me a set tomorrow.'

'That's all right, use mine till then. Well, see you.'

'Where to?'

'My favourite hill.'

'Hill? Didn't they warn you about going off alone?' Rosita's expression was strained.

'Oh, heavens!' cried Lily in mock exasperation. 'Not you, too? Listen, what is everyone going on about? I'm not a child.'

Rosita lifted a finger ominously. 'Really, Lily, you should be more prudent. Paddy's death was not pleasant – have you forgotten? Somir's dangerous!'

'You once loved excitement,' Lily reminded.

'Perhaps, but I'll be forty-two soon, and feeling it.' Lily looked slightly amused at the fuss everyone was making.

'You think it's funny?' Rosita tilted her head.

'No,' she smiled, 'it's just that this "Somir-the-Ripper" stuff has got out of hand.'

'Okay, have it your way,' Rosita showed two palms in defence, 'but at least have a cookie before you go.'

Lily took her hand. 'I know you mean well, Rosita, but my happiness is so supreme, even if anything were to happen to me, my soul will be free; free to love Danny, to honour God for returning him to me.'

'Don't talk like that, girl! And the day before your future spouse arrives!'

Lily blushed, pinched Rosita's cheek playfully, and sailed out of the room.

The A.C. generator had forcefully kicked out the kerosene and gas lamps. It droned significantly behind the parlour. The sound lent an industrial quality to the once grave-quiet village, and many reflected how it certainly had been a messy job trimming lamp-wicks, and using kerosene, or paraffin. Older folk bemoaned the death of peace, and cast remarks about empty vessels. However, soon as the generator's efficiency was established, all lamps were buried in junk boxes, and hands were dusted with a solemn 'Amen!' One woman gazing with fascination at the prodigious machine asked a fellow onlooker, 'Boy, it really deafening; ah shock from dat would kill you dead, dead, noh?' and stared at the thing which could light up an entire village – deaf to the intelligence she sought.

Then the generator broke down, and wives frantically searched their oily junk boxes, sucking their teeth and swearing that 'these new things owny fancy, but dey ain fit a fart!'

On the hill, Lily met the Mahdia Patrol.

'Morning, Miss,' saluted John, Lily's most troublesome pupil. 'You can stay up here. It safe.'

'It is safe,' corrected Lily. 'Anyway, John, I expect it would be.' At that they marched away, swinging their arms mightily.

The wind lifted her hair. She stood entranced by the distant mountains that had been Danny's source of inspiration. Before her they lay, sleeping in the sunshine, and suddenly she felt like crying. She closed her eyes, praying that Danny would appear when she opened them, but quickly admonished herself, and begged forgiveness for seeking His aid for a selfish purpose.

She sat on the grass and recaptured those moments they had spent here, tried to picture Danny's perplexity when he kissed her. Quietly she began to recite his poem:

> 'Love is strength on a lonely day,
> Hope when despair points the way, ...'

She felt trepidation at the thought of their reunion, but assured herself that if he needed encouragement she would sacrifice pride, everything, and fling herself into his arms. But what if she didn't recognise him? No, she was being stupid. Had he changed, though?

Foremost in her thoughts was marriage. To be a mother. To have chubby babies to cuddle, and love – to call her own; a family to cherish! This was the zenith of her dreams.

She was deliberating how she would care for them when a loud fluttering near the condemned buildings startled her. She glanced round. Something had alarmed the birds now flying agitatedly from the trees. She sat up, and felt her pulse racing. Something scurried through the leaves in the undergrowth, and a cold sweat broke out on her forehead. One house under the trees leaned like an unholy creature from the dead. Perhaps it was an opossum, she consoled herself, but her legs felt insecure when she stood up. Nothing moved. She looked around for the patrol. The road was deserted. Another bird squawked and took off in a flurry, bringing fresh terror to Lily. Her heart was beating audibly. The bird left a single, naked, limb quivering. The wind had gone.

She contemplated flight, and might have run if a peccary, wild cow, anything, had come thundering out of the bushes, but the unearthly silence nailed her to the ground! She was about to ridicule herself for being a coward when Somir burst into view.

She stood transfixed. Somir, in rags, his hair matted, his eyes staring, red and swollen, advanced like a servant of the diabolical. In his hand he carried a knife.

'My wife – you, my *wife*!' he said, thumbing his chest, his eyes maniacal things with life of their own. She faltered before his stare, but when he was almost upon her, the fear flew from her breast, and she screamed and screamed.

12

The sergeant stood motionless on the pier, his khaki uniform rumpled and sweat-stained after the drive. Oscar stood beside him looking the older for the trip, the back of his shirt bearing the impression of a seat.

They could see the ferry veering towards them, rocking gently but listing leeward, where most of the passengers craned over the rail.

On the stelling, a wide-shouldered, muscular labourer was using an electric drill like a child's cricket bat turned upside down apparently unimpeded by his exceedingly rotund belly; two other workmen were sawing away at greenheart boards, and an apprentice, sweat dripping profusely from his nose and chin, drove six-inch spikes through thick greenheart planks with a sledgehammer. The carpenter-foreman watched with obvious satisfaction. Near a vendor, another workman sat, eating apple-bananas. When the foreman called he sulked, looked away unconcernedly, and grumbled that when he get sick, sick, none ah dem won't mine he.

'But you ad you breakfast haready,' protested the foreman, indignant.

'But if ah hungry, hungry, wha ah muss do?' The man flung his hand as if chasing off the foreman's remark or, perhaps, the foreman.

At length the ferry approached. Oscar pushed to get near the pier. 'See him?' asked an anxious Hopkinson.

'No, I ... don't see. ...,' Oscar tiptoed, shifting his head like a boxer, then, 'Yes! Yes! Look! Heavens, how he's grown! There he is!'

'Which one?' The lawman, infected by Oscar's excitement, moved forward.

'There ... look! The one with the shoulder bag. Look, he's moving towards us, see?' Oscar started to wave.

'Yes, yes, I see him, and he's waving back,' said the sergeant, feeling important at the occasion.

Minutes later Danny and Oscar were hugging, and paying each other compliments while Hopkinson, a wide grin on his face, stood waiting, as if for his turn. Oscar introduced him, and he and Danny shook hands stiffly. Then he lifted a hand and boomed. 'Boys, come and meet Danny Thorne, B.G. scholar.'

Immediately friends of Hopkinson, and those who knew about the brilliant 'underdog' crowded round and extended congratulations.

Noticeable was the sergeant's proud manner. Many thought Danny was his son. Then, suspecting Danny might be tired, he begged that they be excused, and guided Danny through the huddle.

Danny was elated, and reflected that the grind and sacrifices had been worth it. Only one thing remained to crown his triumph. Tomorrow seemed years away! Would they embrace and kiss? Would she have love enough to ignore hundreds of spectators?

'How're Mom and Lily,' he asked.

'Boy, those two are something,' Oscar laughed.

'Especially that girl of yours!' The sergeant then told how Lily had persecuted him while he was preparing the jeep.

'Yes, she and Rosita talk about you all the time,' Oscar complained. Danny smiled. Yes. They would hug and kiss, immune to embarrassment, and the people would cheer.

Oscar booked rooms at the Hotel Moderne. The sergeant said he would bunk at the station, as he had reports to submit.

As planned, they breakfasted early next morning. At the Texaco station, the sergeant – who really knew everyone it seemed – introduced Danny to the proprietor. The man shook Danny's hand with such lethargic gracelessness that the presentation bordered on embarrassment. Danny couldn't tell whether the man was overwhelmed by his credentials, or simply weighing the sergeant's gesture as a suggestion that the gas should be on the house. The only creature that responded to the beery faced proprietor was a mangy dog, which kept falling asleep on the concrete. The man would kick him, and he would rise, walk a metre or two, then flop down again. 'Delays the customers,' moaned the man.

'Mahdia's waiting for you,' said the sergeant, starting the jeep.

'Yes, and Lily most of all,' promised Oscar, lighting his pipe. Danny had almost forgotten about Oscar's pipe.

Two old men sat on a bridge quarrelling. Between them stood a quarter-bottle of XM, and a glass. One said aloud, 'You all can't see? De white people ain' gone yet, an we people owny burning down one another house, and killing up mattee. What gon happen when all de white people gone? Coolie man can run dis country? Black man nah even own a proper cake-shop, he gon run country? But is why ah-you nigger soh dunce, eh?'

His partner leaned away at a good forty-five degrees, and eyed him scornfully through lids half-closed with drink, his lower lip hanging ignominiously. 'You is not a nigger, too? You know you damn presumptuous? You drink up me f-ing rum den turn round and abuse me? Eh?' With that he cuffed the other clean off the bridge, into the wide gutter below.

The sergeant shook his head regretfully. 'It's an everyday affair in Bartica, I'm afraid. Don't worry, they won't kill each other.'

Drenched, the unfortunate man clambered out of the gutter, hurried to his seat, poured a drink, and gulped. Hopkinson drove off. Danny laughed. 'Never saw a man sober up so quickly!'

Punctuality was never a Guyanese motto, but if word got round of a free cinema matinee and the doors were to be opened at, say four-fifteen, you could safely wager your life that by three o'clock the cinema owners would have to call in the riot squad. Similarly, if a young man possessed the latest 'K' shoes, or gabardine, and was invited to a fete, one outstanding idiosyncrasy is that he would arrive hours early to strut around the square like Rudolph Valentino until sweat, fatigue and impatience drove him to his host.

Whether it was the suspense of waiting to see Mahdia applauding as Danny entered like a triumphant Caesar, or some happy recollection of lovers joyfully flung into each other's arms, the sergeant drove that little bit faster, and soon the jeep was miles away from the mining town.

Not long after their departure, a commotion broke out on the stelling. One man was shouting boisterously and others were holding open mouths in reactions that betrayed shock. 'What?' A man dropped a sledgehammer, and his eyes rolled. '*What* you say?'

The one who had started the tumult, answered by increasing the volume of his transistor. A hush ensued as everyone digested the news that the Sun Chapman had been blown to bits in the Demerara River, extinguishing the lives of over thirty people. Everyone looked about to see how others were taking it, but mirrors would have revealed the best impressions.

An Indian vendor whose son had been beaten to death in Georgetown swore that it only meant 'couple niggers less!'

The tragic news swept through the town, darkening the day. A few vowed never to travel by ferry thereafter. The semi-drunk who ordered a double-rum and swore an oath that 'coolie blood got to spill,' was merely echoing the inevitable, for then, few had the composure to investigate anything. If a negro died, Indians were responsible, the converse also being true. Everyone walked the razor's edge. It was as if they were waiting for it … something, to happen.

The wheel hit a rock, bouncing them in the seat, and they laughed, as they laughed at every jerk, or overhead branch they ducked to avoid, though one or two holes almost brought down Danny's intestines.

An agouti with its short pea-fowl tail hopped across the track, displayed some reddish coat, then vanished; a big-eyed marsupial, a nocturnal poultry terror, peeped from his haunt, and the large wings of a harpy beat authoritatively somewhere in the forest.

After crossing the suspension bridge, the sergeant

pulled over to answer a call of nature. Danny, hearing the man's urine pouring on the leaves, suddenly felt the urge, too. Presently, Oscar joined them.

'He's nearly as tall as you, Hoppy,' Oscar shouted, impressed with Danny's new stature. Hopkinson glanced back. He had heard much about Danny. That he was quiet, sensitive, and intelligent. A few insisted he was coy, but Sam was convinced he was 'crack.'

'I mean,' he had once appealed to Hopkinson, 'who cares about hieroglyphs?'

Hopkinson observed that Danny was profoundly affected by nature, moved almost to stupor; that his was not the academic's approach. He didn't pontificate, or categorise with big words. His appreciation of beauty hinted at the heart of a connoisseur. Strange, he thought, for Danny was into science!

Danny walked over to the precipice, and gazed down at the dense forest growth. Hopkinson decided it was now or never; he had to find out!

'I know you're proud of him, Oscar, but I've often wondered. How come you chose black?'

Oscar eyed him doubtfully.

'You know,' he glanced at Danny. 'I'm surprised no one asked me this before. It's a perfectly normal question.

'Well, my folks died when I was four. Mom was the last to go. Before she died, she begged Miss Goodman, our servant, to look after me. She didn't want me going into an orphanage, you understand, but finances were low, and it was entirely up to the old lady. Well, she kept me.

'I don't know what my parents ever did for her, but she struggled to keep the two of us going, in spite of her ailing back, and rheumatism. We had hard times, you hear, but she never let up, and missed meals so that I might eat ...'

Danny's approach caused Oscar to cut the conversation by asking, 'If you were in my shoes, with a barren wife, what would you have done?'

'All right,' boomed Hopkinson, clapping Danny on the back, 'Let's go meet that fairy of yours. The suspense must be killing her.'

And me, too, Danny wanted to say.

'Any bets?' Oscar nudged Hopkinson, 'Lily will be the first to reach him.'

Danny looked away shyly. Hopkinson wasn't sure. 'Women are funny. Sometimes she goes and dresses up like the flipping Queen of Sheba, and tries to appear unaffected while her heart is fluttering like a trapped eagle.'

Danny applauded the simile, and they laughed, but inside he felt uncontrollable excitement. He knew that every minute the jeep was drawing him closer to Mahdia, closer to her arms. Powerful emotions swirled within. His will – a will that had grown mighty over the years – watered down into a still, mirror-like pond waiting to be rippled. Waiting for the warm puff that would transmit waves of ecstasy through his body.

Something melted in his stomach, and his toes kept contracting, curling automatically as if independently urging on the jeep, and tiny like-charged wires, responding to the sharp impetus of anxiety, touched and sparked in his brain.

Whenever the sergeant yelled, 'Seventeen miles to go,' or 'Only six miles more,' Danny's excitement fuse burned that shorter.

'Don't forget to thank the people for the reception when you see her,' Oscar whispered, 'her beauty may jar your memory.'

'Is she – the same?'

Oscar seemed to digest this, then said, 'No, more beautiful.'

The blood pumped into Danny's face as the jeep negotiated the last narrow passage, and dead ahead lay the last stretch to Mahdia!

He glanced to see if the men could hear the pounding, for his chest now housed a thousand hearts, and even the loud sawing of tyres and the roaring engine, could not drown their almighty beat.

The miracle of 'We've reached!' dawned upon him, as the first cow, the first burning pile of rubbish, came into view, and there, before them stood the first building. It was deserted, but its occupants were probably toasting with the others, waiting impatiently. The jeep sped past the ivy-adorned house.

Then came the village proper! The great WELCOME HOME banner stood out in the distance, hanging majestically across the road, and two bicycles were parked on their stands, but there was not a single sign of human life!

'What the hell's going on?' cried a truly disappointed Hopkinson, half-raising out of the seat to see. Oscar was astonished. His brows twisted as thoughts flashed back and forth in his mind. Hopkinson was first to see the crowd. A hundred-odd people flocking the cottage, poking to see inside, murmuring.

'Christ!' he hissed. The banner flashed past overhead. He braked hard and the jeep's fender crashed into the wicket gate, slamming it shut, hitting out a stave, but even that report failed to turn any of the heads pushing to get a glimpse of whatever was inside the cottage. Danny and Oscar were out in a flash.

They plunged through the crowd, pushing one or two aside roughly in the process, while exclamations of 'He come back! Danny come back!' rose all around. Some turned to stare. Through their bedroom door they saw Rosita leaning over the bed, and there, in as helpless a form as Danny ever saw, lay Lily.

He rushed in. Outside the people were whispering, 'They shoulda track down Somir, and catch he.' 'God, how he could stab up Lily so bad?'

Rosita quickly took Oscar's hand, her eyelashes moist, and urged him out.

'But I want to …' he protested.

'No!' she pleaded, crying openly now. 'Let them be! Lily's losing a lot of blood. She wants to be with him.'

'Where's the lorry?' cried Hopkinson.

'In Bartica. We've just radioed for a doctor. He should be here soon'.

As she moved away. Rosita closed the door after her.

Danny looked down at Lily and the memory of every moment they shared came back to him. Her lips moved. He threw himself on his knees, listening. She spoke again, smiling, and large tears coursed down her temples.

'It's me … Danny.' He swallowed hard.

'Smile for me.' Her voice broke and he burst out, 'No, Lily, I love you. You're all I have.'

'It's His will,' she muttered.

'*Jesus!*' His scream tore through the house, and he buried his head in her arms, blinded by tears. Then he heard it. The voice he had always known whispering, pleading.

'Remember … I love roses, … and only you.'

It was drizzling, and there was hanging over Mahdia a hush too great for many to bear when a small girl climbed the steps and rapped on the door. The cripple himself opened it. 'Yes?'

'She's dead, Mr Savory.'

Ben nodded. 'Thank you. No, no, don't cry, child, please.' He wrapped the tiny girl in his arms and his own tears rolled down her back.

13

After the funeral Danny said little, and avoided those curious about the shootings and burnings in the city. At every opportunity, he visited the hill, and on those quiet days when grey clouds dimmed the sun, when the wind swayed the boughs of trees, or gently rattled a distant zinc sheet, his soul and Lily's would unite. And he would relate, as was her dying request, his thoughts of the mountains, the streams, the valleys, and the wild orchids. Of his love he forever confessed, and sometimes, he begged her to forgive him for harbouring doubts, and whenever he remembered how he had tortured her by not replying to her letters he would cup his face and weep. Once, he couldn't explain, he felt an unnatural closeness to her, her spirit perhaps, and it made him pure, and whole.

Somir had not meant to kill her, but her screaming had become overbearing, excruciating. Why was she afraid? Why did she want to run from him? She was his wife! Don't scream! Blast! People were shouting and running up the road. Stop it, you hear! Stop your damn screaming! You – my wife!

But she wouldn't listen. He held her arms, shook her, begged her to escape with him, but she struggled, and kept screaming. Then the blasted peasantry were coming at him with cutlasses and sticks! He lashed out with his knife blindly – three times.

Then he ran. Through the bushes like a beast clawing the earth, lashing aside the branches, dodging like a soldier being fired on. He ran zig-zag, heading for the swamp. He didn't mean to stab her. God, he didn't mean to! Try as he might he could not shake off the people. And the noise! Then he heard a loud report, and dogs! They were hounding him like a beast! The baying increased. The swamp! Once he reached the swamp he was safe. A palm tree stood out ahead. He laughed, in spite of himself. He was safe. The swamp was near.

He slipped, collapsed in a soft clump of leaves, and scrambled up cursing. Another shot! Missiles ripped into the leaves, the trees, and something like fire flew through his calf. They wanted his blood. God! they wanted his blood! Then he saw it.

He splashed through the musky water, his arms paddling furiously. Finally, his feet shreded by thorns, his calf bathed in blood, he reached the other side, but the dogs kept coming, closing the gap.

He half-ran, half-hopped towards his lair, gasping, and his leg buckled. He fell into a moist accumulation of rotting vegetation. Even as he hit the ground many needles punctured his flesh, and wet, clammy things wriggled about him, slithery bodies with tiny fangs.

Years ago, Somir had seen the victim of a similar curse. He sprang up screaming. Fear turned him back. Towards the guns and dogs of his pursuers. Better sudden death than this! He jumped uncaring into the black, pulpy water, his lungs bursting with the unholy scream of the damned. And this effort spilled fresh blood from the pin-holes in his face and neck.

They saw him charging towards them, the whites of his eyes suffused with streaks like lava, and the men stopped dead in their tracks. Only the dogs pressed on, and Serwall squeezed the trigger when Somir was a metre away.

Across the swamp, little labarias slid under smelly forest debris, huddling near the gnarled buttress of a tree, while their mother, her body arching and curving, coiled around them, vexed over their rudely disturbed siesta.

They saw him coming, a garland of roses in his hands.

'Ah wonder who he is?' whispered a bony woman and both she and her equally gaunt counterpart watched the tall, clean-shaven man as he opened the creaky cemetery gate.

'Morning, comrade,' they hailed him servilely as they picked the choicest daisy bush.

'Morning,' he said, and pressed on. He stopped when he came to a grave set apart from the others, one which bore the epitaph:

HERE LIES MAHDIA'S FLOWER.

Stooping, he stood the flowers against the tombstone, and closed his eyes, remaining thus for a considerable time much to the annoyance of the cronies dying to unravel the mystery.

At last he got up, and left. Instantly, they hoisted their long, darned skirts, and limbered over the muddy ground to the tomb. The one examined the expensive wreath and sighed; the other read the inscription and frowned.

'Girl, you can remember any Lily Serwall what used foh live here?'

'Serwall? Oooh, yes. I hear dat name, but dat was a long, long time … wait! I wonder if … but no, it can't be he.'

'He, who?' cried the first in exasperation.

The other was silent, for she remembered the story of the love that had ended in disaster. She squinted towards the hill, and yes, there he was. The old woman smiled to display one large, yellow tooth. Then she was solemn. 'Come, don't leh we disturb dis girl; she soul must be sleeping in peace, now.'

> 'And I shall hear,
> Though soft you tread above me,
> And all my grave will warmer, sweeter
> be …'

The Dragon Can't Dance

Earl Lovelace

All the year round Aldrick lives in the Calvary Hill slums of Port Spain, waiting for the two days of Carnival, when he will parade and dance in pride and triumph in his resplendent Dragon costume. But this year is different. How can he prevent seventeen-year-old Sylvia from selling herself to rich, middle-aged Mr Guy for the sake of a Carnival costume?

Aldrick and Sylvia are just two of the colourful characters in this brilliant novel by the author of *While Gods Are Falling*.

'This novel is a landmark, not in the West Indian, but in the contemporary novel. ... Nowhere have I seen more of the realities of a whole country disciplined into one imaginative volume.'

C. L. R. James in *Race Today Review*

'A tough, sharply written book which rewards careful reading.'

Trinidad Express

Drumbeat   26
ISBN 0 582 64231 0